MURDER AS STICKY AS JAM

A GLUTEN-FREE MYSTERY

DIANA ORGAIN

Lemonade Press

OTHER TITLES BY DIANA ORGAIN

Third Time's a Crime If only love were as simple as murder…

In dedication to
Flora

CHAPTER 1

Soft jazz played in the background as Mona Reilly bustled around the empty shop. In just a few days, in time for the Memorial Day weekend, would be the grand opening of her shop *Jammin' Honey*, but only if she finished the prep work in time.

Memorial Day weekend was the official opening of the summer tourist season in the scenic mountain town of Magnolia Falls. Mona knew it would be the perfect time to open the doors to the shop that had been only a dream a few months ago. Tucking a strand of glossy black hair behind her ear, she sat down at the café table by the window to catch her breath.

Picking up the Magnolia Falls Gazette, she read the report on the front page about the grand opening. Pride filled her chest with warmth as she read the article once more. She couldn't believe this was happening.

It's real, Mona thought, her nerves kicking up a notch.

A pair of tourists stopped out front and peeked through the window. Mona jumped to attention; her shop was supposed to open in a few days. She had to get a move on.

Where's Vicki? Mona wondered.

It was a quarter past ten and she hadn't heard from her best friend and business partner, Vicki Lawson. Vicki was an organic beekeeper and was the honey part of *Jammin' Honey*. Mona reached for her cell phone to call Vicki, but the phone buzzed in her hand before she could dial.

She saw from the caller I.D. that it was her Great Aunt Beatrice. She'd been able to finally finance the opening of her shop through a generous loan from her Great Aunt Cecilia, Beatrice's identical twin. The two Aunts were identical in everything except the way they handled money, and now Mona cringed at that the thought that Aunt Bee was calling to impose some sort of financial frugality.

"Hello Aunt Bee," Mona said into the phone.

"Mona! Is everything ready?" Bee asked, her voice cracking with enthusiasm.

"Just about. Putting on the finishing touches, you know."

"Cecilia will be very proud."

"I'm sorry she won't be at the opening," Mona said.

Her Great Aunt Cecilia had shocked everyone declaring that, as a celebration for her 80th birthday, she'd be traveling around the world on an exclusive cruise with her new beau, Herman. Herman was a spry and debonair seventy-year old, and Beatrice swore the man was only after Cecilia's money.

As if in a show of defiance, Cecilia had loaned Mona the seed money to open her shop, further annoying Beatrice who firmly believed that everything in life should be a struggle; that which doesn't kill you makes you stronger, was her motto.

Of course, Beatrice had opted to stay in Magnolia Falls and celebrate in her own way, saying that a cruise was way too extravagant, not to mention expensive.

"Are you going to make us a coupon for opening night?" Beatrice asked.

Mona laughed. Bee ran a coupon clipping club. Her frugal reputation preceded her. She was notorious for working over every business owner in the community and hustling discounts for all her members.

"What do you suggest?" Mona asked.

"BOGO," Bee said eagerly.

Mona chuckled. "If I offer buy-one-get-one on opening night, I'll be out of business before the party's even over."

"Okay," Bee said reluctantly. "How about a BOGO on your special blackberry ginger jam?"

Mona glanced at her shelf stocked with jams. There weren't enough blackberry ginger jars to run a special, but if she made a few more batches, she could accommodate Aunt Bee.

"For you, I'll do it," Mona said.

"Ah! You are a dear. I've got the coupons already printed."

"What? You printed the coupons before I even agreed?"

Aunt Bee cleared her throat. "No. Of course not. I only meant you could consider it as good as done."

Mona laughed. "You're a terrible liar."

Bee giggled. "Well, I can guarantee the whole club will be there opening night. And that's another thing I wanted to speak to you about. Don't go all crazy on that party. No need for caterers, or a band or whatever you've got planned. Just put up a few balloons."

Mona winced. There was no way she was going to hold back on her party. She'd been dreaming about opening the shop for too long. She looked around at the hardwood floors, the cherry trim, the glass cases and brass lined counters. It all screamed that no expense had been spared. The shop had a vintage yet modern look. It was a cheerful environment that she knew would be a success.

"Well, you know what Cee says, it takes money to make money," Mona said through a smile.

Bee let out a high-pitched scream, "Don't listen to that old bag! She knows nothing."

Mona giggled. "I knew that'd get your goat. I have to go now, Bee. I have to make some more jam for your coupon clippers."

She hung up and hightailed it to the back of the shop where she plugged in a small burner. As she measured out the water to boil, her cell phone buzzed again.

It was Vicki. Mona poured the water into the pan and answered the phone.

3

"Hey, what's up? Where are you? I was getting worried," Mona said.

"Sorry! I should have called you earlier, but I got a little carried away here at home and made an extra batch of honey lip balm and honey candles, just in case."

"Just in case, in case of what?"

"What if we sell out? I don't want the shelves to be empty on our grand opening weekend, do you?"

"My Aunt Bee called you, didn't she?" Mona asked.

Vicki chuckled. "Yeah, I agreed to a—"

"Two for one special?"

Vicki moaned. "You too?"

"I'm just starting another batch of my blackberry ginger jam," Mona said.

"Oh," Vicki said. "I thought you were already at the store?"

"I am. I brought my portable hot plate," Mona said.

"Well don't burn the shop down!" Vicki said.

"Come on," Mona laughed. "I'm not that stupid!"

"Okay, I'll be there soon. I'll bring breakfast," Vicki said. "Biscuits and coffee sound good?"

"You know me too well. In the meantime, I'll be here all alone, working my hands to the bone."

Vicki laughed. "I know you're such a workaholic! Anyway, I'm going to make it up to you."

"Yeah, well coffee and biscuits will only get you so far. I need you to scrub the bathroom and stock shelves."

"I know," Vicki said and by the tone of her voice Mona could tell she was smiling, "But I have another little surprise for you."

Mona gripped the phone tightly. She hated surprises. "What's that?"

"Leo is coming for the grand opening," Vicki said, giggling as she hung up.

"Wait! Wait!" Mona said into the dead phone. She stared at the phone in her hand, trying not to hyperventilate.

Leo's coming to the grand opening?

Leo Lawson, Vicki's older brother, was tall, dark and handsome. He'd been the first boy Mona had a crush on back in school, and she'd never gotten over him. In high school, he'd broken her heart when he started dating, Lacey, the head cheerleader. But shortly after graduation, he'd left Magnolia Falls, to join the military, and now he was back after eight long years.

She knew he worked at the Magnolia Falls PD, but she hadn't seen him, yet.

Not properly anyway.

She'd ducked out of the grocery store a few times, when she'd seen his patrol car pull into the parking lot. And there'd been the time, she snuck out of the back of the bookstore on Main Street, when she'd heard his voice asking the clerk for the latest police procedural.

But she hadn't spoken with him, yet.

She'd been in the hospital with tonsillitis during his homecoming party, and she'd missed him twice at Vicki's due to bad timing.

As she waited for the water to boil, she printed out the inventory list and the pricing guide and headed back to the shop. With a pricing gun in her hand, she priced all the blackberry jam and then began working on the strawberry. Thoughts of Leo filled her mind and she daydreamed about seeing him at the grand opening.

What am I going to wear? Mona thought in a panic.

Looking around the shop, she wondered if she would have time to go shopping and pick out something new and sexy before Friday. Jammin' Honey was filled with half empty shelves, boxes of jams, jellies, honey candles, lotions and balms everywhere, she doubted she would have time to sleep much less go on a shopping trip.

She hummed along with the music and priced the merchandise to the beat, invigorated by the thought of the grand opening and Leo. When the phone in her apron pocket vibrated. She answered it without glancing at the caller ID.

"I knew you couldn't stay away. Are you bringing me lunch instead of breakfast?" asked Mona.

"Excuse me?" asked the voice on the phone.

Mona realized it wasn't Vicki, she looked at the phone and saw that the caller was Lacey MacInroy from the bakery.

"Lacey, I'm sorry, I thought you were someone else."

"Obviously," said Lacey in a condescending tone, "I need to meet with you at once, can you come by the bakery before lunch?"

"Lacey, this isn't a great time. I have so much to do before the Grand Opening. Can you just tell me what's going on over the phone?"

"I only called because this is important. It affects the catering menu for the Grand Opening. One of my suppliers has informed me that he's out of that gluten-free almond flour you wanted, so I've had to make a few last-minute changes. I think you'll find the substitutions suitable, but I need your approval before I can proceed," explained Lacey in a tone that Mona felt sure betrayed the fact that Lacey was rolling her eyes.

"I'm sure whatever you substitute will be fine, as long as it's gluten-free," Mona said.

Lacey made a clucking noise in the back of her throat. Clearly, she was put out by Mona's request. It had been a struggle to get Lacey to agree to cater the event at all, much less make it gluten-free. But, after the great write up in the Magnolia Falls Gazette, Mona had been able to persuade her.

"Do you really need me to come right now?" Mona asked. "I'm in the middle of prepping the shop, and I have so much left to do. Can I just give you my approval over the phone?'

"Not if you want me to cater this affair. I must have you taste the final recipe. I need to know that you will be pleased with the pastry selections, and this morning is the only time I have available."

Mona stuffed down her impatience. Lacey's bakery was the only caterer in town and with only few days left before the grand opening, she didn't have the time or energy to make enough food for the event. Obviously, Lacey wasn't giving her a choice.

With a sigh, Mona said, "Give me ten minutes. I'll be right over."

"Fine," answered Lacey.

Mona was about to say goodbye, but Lacey had already hung up.

She slipped the phone into her jeans pocket and tried not to think about how infuriating Lacey was. Pulling the apron over her head, she vowed not to let Lacey's attitude ruin her day. Despite the inconvenience of having to stop work and test drive a few pasties at her caterer's insistence, the day was going well. If she kept working at her present pace, all her stock would be ready to sell by the weekend.

Walking to the back, she was tempted to burst out in song. She loved everything about her new shop, it was truly a dream come true; thanks to Aunt Cee's investment and belief in her.

She turned off the burner and unplugged it for safe measure.

Aunt Bee's coupon clippers would have to wait for their special, at least for the moment. Then, sliding her purse onto her shoulder, she walked out of the store and locked the front door.

THE BELL ABOVE THE DOOR CHIMED CHEERFULLY AS MONA WALKED INTO the bakery. A quick glance at her watch confirmed that there was no time to spare in her hectic schedule for this last-minute errand. Checking off the items on the endless to do list was Mona's priority, not placating the caterer.

Fresh baked bread and sweet pastries crowded the glass cases, and their aroma combined to create a decadent ambrosia. Mona inhaled the soothing scent, surprised that a woman as cold as Lacey MacInroy could create warm and delicious baked goods.

"Can I help you?" asked a freckle-faced young man.

Glancing at her watch once more, Mona answered, "I'm here to see Lacey."

The man disappeared behind the door that said *Kitchen*.

The door swung open, and a woman wearing a white apron over tailored capris and a crisp pink polo greeted Mona, "Mona, please join me in the kitchen."

As Mona crossed toward the kitchen door, Lacey smiled and

wiggled her fingers in a friendly wave at an older gentleman waiting in line. With her shoulder length honey-blond hair pulled back in a ponytail and only a hint of bronzer on her cheeks, Lacey appeared to be as fresh faced and beautiful as she had been in high school.

That's Lacey, everyone's friend except mine.

Whatever did I do to get on her bad side?

Lacey's warm smile disappeared as the kitchen door closed behind them.

"Do you have any idea how difficult it has been to find that gluten-free flour you wanted?" Lacey asked with a frown.

The grand opening was only days away, and Mona didn't want risk upsetting Lacey. If the caterer backed out now Mona didn't know what she would do.

Mona met Lacey's frown with a smile, it wasn't sincere, but it was the best she could muster under the stress. "Lacey, I don't understand why your supplier was out of this flour, gluten-free is popular. My request wasn't that unusual, I have seen that flour at all the big grocery chains."

"That's just it, it's very trendy, so every bakery from San Francisco to New York is using it for wedding cakes, breads, you name it. My supplier told me I should have ordered it over two weeks in advance."

I tried to book your catering service for over a month.

Hiding her frustration, Mona tried a different approach and said diplomatically, "I appreciate your efforts to find a solution. You said you may have found a suitable substitute?"

Opening a drawer, Lacey pulled out a card that was covered in neat rows of handwriting. Handing the card to Mona she asked, "What do you think of the recipe? I can use half gluten-free almond flour I found at the health food market and half gluten-free self-rising flour."

"What's in the self-rising flour, and will it taste the same?" asked Mona.

Mona planned to offer samples of her jams and Vicki's honey along with the pastries. They had to be good!

"Garbanzo beans, ground fava beans, it sounds disgusting, but by the time it's all mixed up, no one can tell the difference," Lacey answered.

Mona was certain that she would be able to tell a difference between almond flour and ground beans, but it was too late to argue over ingredients. Stuck between a rock and a hard place, she was almost willing to agree to the changes in the recipe when a question popped into her head, "If you could find almond flour at the health food market, why can't you buy enough of that to use instead of using it for half of the recipe?"

Lacey rolled her eyes as she answered, "Do you have any idea how much that stuff costs? I'm already doing you an enormous favor just accepting this job, and now you want me to not make any money on it?"

Her first impulse was to tell Lacey to forget it, instead Mona said, "Lacey, I understand you have to make money, just bill me for the additional amount and please use the good flour, no ground beans."

The tension between them was palpable. In ten years, nothing had changed, Lacey still treated Mona with contempt, when it should have been the other way around, after all Lacey won the heart of Leo.

"Fine, have it your way, but I promise you it will be expensive, and I'll bill you. I don't care if your shop doesn't sell a single jar of jelly, I expect to be paid on time," Lacey snapped as she snatched the card out of Mona's hand and scribbled the changes to the recipe.

Silently seething, Mona wanted to tell Lacey that the deal was off, but common sense prevailed, "Lacey, I'll pay you in advance if that's what you want."

Lacey opened her mouth to answer but was drowned out by the wail of fire-truck sirens.

Forgetting their argument over gluten-free almond flour, the two women stared at each other before Mona said in a loud voice, "That sounded close."

Lacey nodded and walked out of the kitchen followed by Mona.

Stepping onto the red brick sidewalk, Mona was startled when a fire truck with its lights flashing sped past. The sirens were louder outside the bakery, she could smell smoke which meant the fire was really close.

A plume of dark smoke rose only a few blocks from the bakery. Slowly, Mona came to the awful realization that the smoke was coming from the direction of her shop.

Oh God, please no, not Jammin' Honey!

CHAPTER 2

*W*ithout saying a word to Lacey, Mona ran to her car and jumped in the driver's seat. Jamming the gear shift into drive, she tore out of the parking space, driving like a racecar driver speeding towards Jammin' Honey. Praying as she drove, she ran a red light and a stop sign. Frantically hoping that it was not her shop on fire, although she had a sinking feeling with each passing block that she'd arrive to find the place, her dream fully engulfed.

How could this happen?

Fear gripped her heart as she saw a police barricade surrounding the street where *Jammin' Honey* sat. The barricade prevented her from driving any closer to the scene of the fire, but she didn't need to be any closer to realize the awful truth.

My shop is on fire!

Her heart raced, and a wave of nausea broke over her as she parked the car. Flashing red lights, smoke and the crackling of fire consuming her building created a surreal scene that would be etched into her memory for the rest of her life.

Running down the street toward the fire, she was stopped by a police officer she didn't recognize. He held her back from getting any closer to the structure fire that was her lifelong dream being destroyed right in front of her eyes.

"It's my shop," she wailed.

The officer nodded. "Is anyone in there?"

Mona shook her head. "No. Just my...just...my...inventory." Her knees felt weak. "And my recipe book, too."

Yellow and orange flames climbed into the sky, and the smoke carried the sweet scent of sugar, making Mona think of all the boxes of jam in the kitchen and strewn all over the floor of the shop.

Tears spilled from her eyes and fell down her cheeks, as she sunk to her knees on the sidewalk. The police officer helped her to a bench across the street.

"Ma'am, are you going to be alright?" the police officer asked.

Mona was too stunned to answer, she sat still on the bench feeling the weight of his eyes on her.

"Ma'am, if it's any consolation, the fire department is doing everything they can to save it. Is there anyone I can call for you?"

"No, I mean yes, I mean - "Just as Mona was about to say Vicki's name, her voice rang out.

"Mona!" Vicki rushed across the street arms outstretched as she raced to pull Mona into an embrace. "Oh my Lord! I was so scared you were in there! Thank goodness you got out!"

The police officer nodded, glad to see Mona taken care of. "Ma'am, I'll be right over there if you need anything." He walked across the street just as curious onlookers were approaching the scene.

Mona's chest ached with the weight of a broken heart as another fire truck approached.

She gasped as sharp pain assaulted her with a shortness of breath.

Vicki rubbed her back. "You're freezing. Let me get a blanket from my car."

More flames plumed over the top of the building as Vicki ran to her vehicle.

I can't watch this. Mona thought

She turned the other way and saw a group of people gathered

looking at the blaze. It made her nauseous to see everyone staring at the blaze that had just moments ago held so much promise for her.

Using all her strength, she managed to stand, her hand on the bench to steady herself. Her head was swimming, her breath shallow, she knew she should sit back on the bench before she crumpled into a heap on the ground. She dug deep and found a reserve of strength inside.

I won't pass out! She promised herself.

Summoning all her strength, she willed her legs to move forward.

She couldn't sit still. She had to help the firefighters.

Vicki ran back to Mona. "What are you doing? Get back!" She pulled Mona back to the bench and wrapped the crocheted afghan she'd retrieved from her car around Mona's shoulders. "Come on, girl. Don't get all crazy on me. There's no way I'm going to let you run back inside that building. Is that what you were trying to do?"

Mona shook her head. "I wanted to help."

Vicki grabbed Mona's hand. "The best help we can offer is to stay out of the way." Vicki rubbed Mona's fingers. "Honey, you're frozen."

Mona was stunned that she could be cold with an enormous fire in front of her. And yet, she did feel chilled.

Shock.

"When I heard about the fire, I called your cell. But when you didn't answer your phone, I thought you might have been in the shop when it, the fire, happened. I was so worried"

Mona nodded numbly, "I was at Lacey's when it happened. If only I had been in the shop, I could have stopped it. It's all my fault for leaving."

Vicki kneeled down on the pavement by Mona's side and declared, "Mona, you can't say that, if you were there you may have been killed. I'm glad you weren't."

"Vicki, everything is gone. It's horrible," Mona said, tears running down her face.

"Not everything is gone. Not you! Not you or me. That's the important thing. We can start over, honey."

13

"My Aunt Cee's investment … it's …" A wail bubbled up in Mona's throat, and she let her best friend pull her to her chest to cry.

How will I ever repay Aunt Cee now?

After a moment of release Mona managed to say, "How did you hear about the fire?"

Vicki motioned over to the crowd of bystanders. "Alexander called me."

Alexander Kaas was the owner of Magnolia Falls Wine and Cheese shop, *As You Slice It*. Mona and Vicki had worked at the shop for many years before Mona left in the spring to open her own store. Mona turned to the crowd and saw Alexander. There was a grim expression on his face, and he gave her a meek wave.

Mona remembered the day she told him she was leaving to begin her business; he was so mad that he turned bright red. He was furious and told her she had no business experience and her store would fail.

"He was right," Mona said.

"What?" Vicki asked.

"I had no business trying to run a store. Alexander told me the shop would fail and now look—"

Vicki rubbed Mona's back. "Don't say that! This isn't your fault—" Vicki's hand froze mid-way down Mona's back. "Oh … gosh, honey. When you left to go to Lacey's shop … were you making jam—?"

"I turned off the burner! Vicki, I swear," Mona said, a lump forming again in her chest.

I did turn off the burner, didn't I?

THE RIDE HOME WAS A BLUR FOR MONA, THE DETAILS HAZY AS VICKI drove and parked her car in Mona's driveway. Somewhere on the ride home, the deep pain changed and became a numbness that made the events feel unreal. Turning the key in the lock, she pushed open the front door. Her purse fell from her hand onto the kitchen table, the keys left in the lock and Mona collapsed on the couch.

Vicki grabbed the keys out of the lock and followed her inside.

Mona stared up at the ceiling. It was the same as it had been that morning when she left home, the same plain white paint and antique ceiling fan that spun endlessly in circles during the warm months. But so much had changed since the morning she felt somehow offended that the ceiling had the nerve to stay the same.

Mona lay on the couch, unmoving, until Vicki peered over her, blocking Mona's view of the ceiling fan

"Mona!!! Mona, are you in there?" Vicki asked.

"Yup," Mona heard herself answer, but her own voice sounded far away.

"You are seriously as pale as a ghost. Should I take you to the emergency room?"

"I'm fine," Mona answered, quietly.

Vicki kneeled down on the floor beside Mona and declared, "I'm going to make us a couple of stiff drinks. If you don't look like part of the land of the living soon, I'm going to call an ambulance."

"I'm fine," repeated Mona as she made an effort to sit up.

Vicki grabbed the remote control off the coffee table and clicked on the TV. "Let's watch *Competition for the Crown*; you'll feel better when you see some people have it worse than you right now."

"*Competition for the Crown* is fiction, Vicki," Mona whined.

"Still, how you would like to be beheaded for betraying the crown?"

Mona smiled in spite of herself. "There is no crown."

Vicki giggled as she left the room to fix some cocktails. "Well, if there was, I know you'd never betray the crown."

A battle raged on the TV, complete with horse mounted knights slaying each other but Mona could hardly watch her favorite show.

Vicki returned to the room with two lemon-drop martinis in hand. She put the glasses on the coffee table and sat on the couch beside Mona. She muted the TV and said, "I just got a text from my cousin, Doug. He's with the fire department; he thinks it wasn't a total loss, isn't that good news?"

Like a light switch being thrown, Mona suddenly woke out of her stupor, "Not a complete loss?"

Vicki nodded. "See, it's like I always say, everything is going to work out, somehow."

Mona wiped away a tear and said, "I'm so sorry I wasn't there to save our shop, all of the stock went up in smoke—"

"Not all our stock, I made a few batches of lip balm and candles today, and I still have my hives! As long as my Queens are happy ..." She glanced at Mona. "What?"

Mona felt as if she would pass out. "My recipes."

Vicki frowned. "Your recipes? You know those things by heart."

"They were mom's. All I had left of her," Mona choked on a sob as Vicki squeezed her shoulder.

Mona's mother had passed away when Mona was a young girl. Her best memories of her mother were in the kitchen, cooking and laughing. Her mother had taught Mona everything she knew about food preparation, especially making jelly.

She'd cherished the recipe book that had been written by her own mother's hand.

And now it was gone.

"It's not all you had left of her, Mona. She's always going to be in your heart and cooking," Vicki said.

Mona pressed her hands to her head trying to quell the pain.

Vicki straightened. "Anyway, if Doug is right, maybe we can be back in business soon, what do you think?"

Managing a weak smile, Mona answered, "I hope so. Every dollar of my Aunt Cee's loan was tied up in the shop. What are we going to do?"

Mona's cell phone vibrated on the table, both woman leaned in to look at the caller id. "Aunt Bee," Mona groaned, sending the call to voicemail.

Vicki handed her the lemon-drop martini. "Yeah, can't face talking to her right now, huh?"

Mona shrugged took a big swig of the martini. "She's going to give me the, *I told you so*, speech."

The phone immediately buzzed again, and Mona grimaced to see her cousin Stewart's face light up her screen. Stewart had no qualms about letting Mona know he was furious with her for taking Aunt Cee's money. Apparently, he'd been asking Aunt Cee for a loan for a while, and she'd refused.

"You want me to talk to him?" Vicki asked.

Mona shook her head and pressed the red button on the phone, sending Stewart into silence. She swirled the golden liquid in her glass and said, "Well, this helps calm my nerves, but it doesn't do anything about our predicament."

"Keep drinking," Vicki said. "Some idea will hit us."

After a moment, Vicki suddenly jolted forward and raised a finger in an aha gesture. "You know, Alexander said we could always sell our goods in his store," Vicki said.

Mona stiffened. "When did he say that?"

"Remember? When we told him we were opening up shop."

"Because he thought our shop would flop!" Mona said. "I can't stand him, it's as if he willed us to fail!"

"No, he didn't," Vicki said. "He offered us a safety net."

"I'd like to strangle him with that safety net," Mona grumbled.

She found Alexander difficult to deal with. He was temperamental and hot headed, but every time she mentioned that to Vicki, Vicki defended him.

Probably, Mona thought, *the fact that Alexander looks like a Viking stepping off the cover of a Harlequin romance is clouding Vicki's judgment.*

Mona put down her martini glass and was just about to comment on this when she looked over at the TV and saw Leo on the news. He stood next to a blonde reporter with a microphone thrust under his chin. His dark hair and eyes sizzled right through the screen and into her heart. Behind him was smoky rubble, the remains of what had only this morning been *Jammin' Honey*.

She gasped. "Oh my! Where's the remote! Turn on the volume! It's Leo!"

Vicki jumped to grab the remote and accidently toppled her martini glass across the table. Sticky liquid covered the device as she pressed every button.

Mona lurched toward the TV, just as the news flash concluded and a commercial for dishwasher soap took over.

"What in the world?" Mona asked. "Leo was at the fire? Why?"

Her heart beat a mile a minute as she tried to process what his presence there could mean. He was in a police detective that much was true, but he wasn't a fire fighter.

Vicki shrugged. "I don't know. Let me clean up my mess and I'll call him."

Vicki disappeared into Mona's kitchen as the sound of car tires crunching gravel on her driveway filled Mona with panic. It was well after sunset, and she hadn't been expecting anyone. A car door slammed shut and then heavy footsteps on the front steps announced the arrival of an unknown guest.

Mona peered out the front window just as the quiet of the evening was disrupted by a door bell.

Vicki came out of the kitchen with a wet rag in her hand. "Who is it?" she asked Mona, who was frozen at the window. When she didn't get a response, she looked out the peep hole, then swung open the front door. "Hey! Did you come to join the pity party?"

Mona watched with bated breath as the man she loved, her crush for over a decade, walked into her living room. Instinctively, Mona brushed aside a wisp of hair.

Of all the days for Leo to come by, I must look awful. I'm a complete wreck!

"Mona, Vicki, I'm sorry about what happened to your store today," Leo said as he gazed at Mona.

Mona stood in an awkward greeting. "Thank you, Leo, for stopping by. That was nice of you, can I get you anything, tea, coffee, a bite to eat?"

"No, I'm good, I'm still on duty." Then he glanced around the room. "Whoa. It smells like a distillery in here."

Vicki gave her brother a quick hug. "Well you smell like smoke, so

I guess that makes us even. Don't worry. We're still sober, but I spilled my lemon drop martini when we saw you on the news." She proceeded to mop up the table as she asked. "What was that about anyway?"

"I've been assigned this case," he answered. "Do you mind if I sit down?"

Mona blushed as she often did any time she was around Leo, "Sorry, I don't know where my manners have gone."

"It's fine, you have had a hard day," he said, touching Mona's hand for a moment.

A swirl of excitement fired through Mona's veins at his touch, but she fought to contain herself.

Leo looked at her strangely for a moment, as if he wanted to say more, but he released her hand and sank down in the leather club chair beside the sofa, instead.

"What is it, Leo?" Vicki asked.

"I'm afraid that the news I have for you all isn't good; your bad day is about to get worse."

Mona collapsed onto the couch, tears stinging her eyes. She grabbed a throw pillow and pressed her face into it.

She felt on the verge of an ugly cry, but that was the last thing she wanted to do in front of Leo. She took a deep breath and then looked up from the pillow and met his gaze. In her steadiest voice, she said, "I know what you are going to say, the building is gone, right? It's a total loss, isn't it?"

"Leo, please tell us that isn't true, it would take months to rebuild," Vicki said.

Leo shook his head slowly and answered their fears, "I wish it was that, but it's far worse. At first, I thought I would be investigating a fire, but now it looks like arson and homicide."

Mona felt the blood drain from her face, and the room seemed to tilt. She reached out to Vicki and gripped her best friend's hand.

Homicide?

CHAPTER 3

*M*ona turned to Vicki and mouthed, "Murder?"

Vicki was far less subtle, "Leo, that's not possible!" she shouted. "There wasn't anyone there today but Mona."

"The firemen discovered a body in the shop's warehouse," Leo said.

"A body?" Mona repeated, still in shock.

Leo nodded slowly.

Mona frowned. "That can't be right. The warehouse is all boarded up. We haven't even had a chance to clean it ..." She shook her head, trying to process her thoughts.

How could someone have been in the warehouse?

Vicki jumped in to say, "We weren't using the warehouse. It was badly in need of repair."

"It was just me in the shop today, I swear." Mona said. "There wasn't anyone with me."

"You may not have been using your warehouse, but someone was there today," Leo said.

Vicki shook her head and said, "No, Leo. You must have it wrong, we would've known if someone was there."

Mona thought about her morning at the shop and quietly admitted, "Wait Vicki, it might be true, I mean I did have the music on while

I was pricing stock in the front of the store. Someone could have been in the warehouse, and I may not have heard them. I just can't imagine who would have been back there, it was a mess."

Leo provided the answer, "We were able to identify the remains as belonging to Collin MacInroy."

Vicki gasped, and Mona stared at Leo, "Collin was in our warehouse? What in the world was he doing there?"

"Collin MacInroy?" Mona muttered. "Lacey's husband?"

"That can't be right, it just can't be," Vicki said.

Leo shook his head back and forth in silence. "I'm afraid it's true."

A stunned silence fell on the group. Mona knew Collin had been Leo's dear friend in high school. They had served in the military together, but they'd returned home separately and never seemed close again. She studied Leo's face now, full of grief, and she longed to embrace him. Instead, she reached out and brushed his hand.

His jaw tightened, and he gave her a brief nod.

Vicki had no reservations, she wrapped Leo in a bear hug and said, "No. Leo! Not Collin. I'm so sorry!"

Leo stiffened under his sister's hug, and he uncoiled himself from her grip. He stood. "I have to find out why he was there," Leo said.

"I was at Lacey's bakery today when the fire broke out," Mona said. "She called me and, pretty much, insisted that I go over immediately to meet with her.

"Meet with her for what?" Vicki asked.

"She said I had to approve a recipe, how weird is that, I was at her bakery when her husband was in the warehouse, that can't be a coincidence, can it?" asked Mona.

"That is interesting," Leo said, pulling out a small notebook from the breast pocket of his uniform. "I have to take a statement about your whereabouts today and the events of the morning, are you prepared to do that tonight?"

Vicki and Mona exchanged glances, and Mona sighed.

The news of Collin's death in her warehouse was more than Mona could handle for one day, she turned to Leo, "You're the officer in charge of this case, if I need to make a statement tonight, I'll do that for you, but I can't think anymore—"

"I can swing by in the morning." Leo offered.

"If it can wait until tomorrow, I'd be grateful," Mona said.

Leo nodded and put the notebook back into his pocket. "It's been a tough day for all of us," he said, standing. "How does seven tomorrow morning sound?"

"Seven will be fine, I'll make sure I'm awake," Mona said.

Leo turned to Vicki. "Vicki, are you going to be okay?"

"I'll be okay." She glanced at Mona and gave her a reassuring smile. "We both will."

Mona grimaced but said nothing.

Vicki turned back to her brother. "Do you need a statement from me, too?"

"I'll call you tomorrow and arrange for one of the other officers to take your statement, since I'm your brother. I don't want anyone accusing me of having a conflict of interest."

Vicki nodded. "Okay. If you need me, I'm staying here with Mona tonight." She leaned over and gave Mona's knee a squeeze.

"No problem," Leo said.

Mona started to stand to see Leo out, but he stopped her.

"Don't get up," Leo said. "You've been through a lot today, get some rest and I'll see you tomorrow."

"I'll walk you out," Vicki said.

Mona waved at them, "See you later," she called to Leo as he left.

Vicki closed the front door softly behind them, and Mona was left alone in her living room.

Arson and murder.

Those words replayed over and over in her head as she lay on the couch and pulled the afghan over her head. Willing herself to wake up, she found that she wasn't dreaming.

This wasn't a nightmare.

It was all happening, and there wasn't anything she could do to stop it.

<><><>

MONA AWOKE BEFORE DAWN THE FOLLOWING MORNING, SHE HADN'T slept well and the image staring back at her in the bathroom mirror confirmed that. Even the dark bags under her red, puffy eyes had dark bags.

Mona showered, dressed in a pair of jeans and a t-shirt. Brushing her hair, she debated with herself about putting on make-up.

Do I want to look like I'm trying to get his attention?

Settling for tinted moisturizer, a dab of concealer, and a swipe of berry lip stick, she walked out of the bathroom and joined Vicki in the kitchen.

Vicki greeted her with a smile, "Good morning, I made a pot of coffee."

"What would I do without you?"

"This morning you might have to find out, I've to get back to the farm, my chickens and honey bees are probably wondering where I am."

Mona tried not to panic. She hadn't planned to be alone with Leo, "Vicki, can't they wait until after Leo leaves, I mean, after I give my statement?"

Vicki slid her purse onto her shoulder and hugged Mona as she said, "I wish I could stay, but I need to get home to see about the chicks; they are accustomed to their freedom at five a.m. and I'm already overdue."

"I understand, call me later."

"I sure will, bye!" Vicki waved as she walked out the door.

Mona poured a cup of coffee and sat down at the kitchen table. She glanced at the clock on the wall and realized that it was quarter to seven, and Leo would be there any second. Her heart raced, and she was overcome with anxiety.

Managing to convince herself that she was over Leo all those years he was in the army, Mona wasn't prepared for his return. It was easier

23

to lie to herself about her true feelings when Leo was on the other side of the world and not seated across from her. Drinking coffee in her kitchen, her hands trembling, she hated to admit it, she was still in love with Leo.

She ran to her bedroom and looked at the reflection in the mirror, she suddenly didn't like what she was wearing. Staring at the clothes in her closet, she fretted about what to wear.

Her cell phone vibrated on her nightstand, and she jumped for it. Maybe Leo was calling to cancel.

The screen told her it was Aunt Bee again. She hesitated, if she didn't pick up, Aunt Bee would be on her doorstep soon, and yet, did she really have the energy to talk to her Aunt right now, when Leo would be here any minute?

The doorbell rang, it was too late to change or talk to Aunt Bee. She sent her into voicemail and raced out to the front room.

Mona opened the door to find Leo standing on her front porch gazing at the mountains in the distance. He spoke in a hushed tone, "The view from your porch is magnificent. I missed the mountains when I was in the desert."

Mona stepped out of her house and joined him, "That is one reason I stayed in town. I don't think anywhere else in the world could rival this."

They stood side by side, gazing at the green mountains rising into the low hanging clouds of the morning sky. Neither spoke in that tranquil moment, but the thoughts swirling in Mona's head didn't let her enjoy the moment.

Leo was standing beside her, her heart ached to feel his arms around her, his lips on hers, but it was a daydream. Leo had never held her, and she'd never felt his kiss. If anything, he was always fraternal with her, but this misty morning on the porch, she discovered she wasn't over him.

Resisting the urge to throw herself at him, she looked at the mountains instead, waiting for him to speak or act.

"I could stand on your porch for hours, but we have work to do, are you ready?" Leo asked as he tuned to face Mona.

They were only about a foot apart.

It would be so easy to lean in and kiss him.

"Mona, are you okay," Leo asked.

Mona jolted out of her fantasy. "What?"

"Are you ready to give me your statement?"

"Yes, I'm sorry, I didn't sleep well, please, come in," she said. "Vicki made us some strong coffee before she left."

Leo nodded and followed her inside to the kitchen. He sat down at the table and waited patiently for her to pour him a cup.

I could get used to looking at him, Mona thought. *He looks like he belongs here.*

He belongs with me.

She placed the coffee on the table in front of him and asked, "How do you take it?"

"Black is fine. Just a word of warning, this is going to be informal, so I may have to ask you to come to the station in the future as things come up, do you understand?"

"Sure," Mona replied as she sat down.

"Good, let's get started. I need to ask you a few questions to get the ball rolling in this investigation. You were the only other person in the shop yesterday. Any details you can provide will help me solve this case and find out what happened to Collin."

"Collin, I'm struggling not to think about that, I had nightmares about it last night when I tried to sleep. How is Lacey, I mean, how is she taking it?"

Leo answered, "I'm not supposed to talk about this, but I'll tell you she's taking it hard, telling her about her husband was difficult."

"I'm sure it was," Mona said as she assessed the situation.

It had been a strange chain of events, Leo had broken her heart when he started dating Lacey. Then right after graduation, he left Lacey and joined the army. Lacey married Collin less than two months later. Although shortly after that. Collin followed in Leo's footsteps and joined the military. Now, he'd died in a fire in Mona's warehouse while she was with Lacey, and Leo was the one to notify her of her husband's death.

"Are you ready to begin?" asked Leo.

"I'm, ready when you are," Mona said as she thought about Lacey and the circumstances surrounding Collin's death.

Was it a coincidence that Collin dies only a few weeks after Leo returns to town?"

"Mona, did you hear the question?" Leo asked.

"Can you repeat it?" Mona asked.

"You told me that Lacey called you just before the fire, is, that right?"

"It is, it should be on my cell phone, in the history."

"Good, I may need to see that at some point in the future, so don't erase it."

"Fine. I have it right here," answered Mona.

"About the warehouse, you and Vicki both said you never used it, tell me about it," prompted Leo.

"The warehouse was part of the shop, but it wasn't renovated, and the roof leaked. It needed some serious repairs and a good cleaning. I had high hopes that it would be stocked full of jams, jellies, and your sister's honey products, but it doesn't look like that is ever going to happen now," Mona said; her throat constricted, and her voice cracked.

Leo looked alarmed, and Mona regretted becoming emotional in front of him. She reached for a napkin to dab her eyes, but Leo pulled a handkerchief from his breast pocket.

"Here," he said, handing her the soft cloth.

Their knuckles bumped, sending an electric jolt through Mona making her cheeks flush. She cleared her throat and nervously wriggled in her chair.

Oh my Lord! I'm an idiot! Get it together, Mona! She thought.

The doorbell rang and startled them.

Oh no!

Aunt Bee!

Leo swiveled in his chair, turning toward the front room. "Are you expecting anyone?"

Mona rose. "It's probably my Aunt Bee."

There's no avoiding her now! What terrible timing she has. I should have returned her calls.

Leo stood with her and walked behind her as Mona crossed the front room and opened the door.

Aunt Bee stood on the porch. Her curly white hair peeked out from under a leopard print cowboy hat. She wore an outrageously bright pink wrap-around skirt and a white blouse with a lacy neckline. Her boots matched the hat. She looked embarrassingly adorable, and Mona cringed while Leo chuckled.

Aunt Bee threw herself into Mona's arms. "My dear! Why haven't you called me? I thought you'd gone up in a puff of smoke!"

Mona squeezed her Aunt. "I'm sorry, Aunt Bee. Forgive me. I'm still slightly in a state of shock."

Aunt Bee untangled herself from Mona and pushed inside the house. She stopped short at seeing Leo. "Oh my goodness. What is this handsome young man doing here?" Aunt Bee wiggled her hips and shoulders and gave Mona a meaningful look.

Oh Lord! Can a hole open up and swallow me whole, please?

Leo smiled. "Hello Aunt Bee. I'm here on official duty I'm afraid."

Aunt Bee gave a pouty face and grabbed his hand. "One day, Mr. Leo Lawson, you're going to realize that my Great Niece is a good catch—"

"That's enough, Aunt Bee," Mona said, her face burning. She rushed to separate her Aunt from Leo.

Aunt Bee giggled. "But I haven't finished telling him how great you are."

Mona said. "We've known each a long time, Aunt Bee—"

"Which means, I know how great Mona is," Leo said, with an easy smile.

Aunt Bee shrugged, undeterred. "Well, maybe. But do you know how head-over-heels in love she—"

Mona coughed over Aunt Bee's last word, and Leo quirked an eyebrow at her.

An awkward silence descended over them, and Mona figured talking about murder was a better option than committing one.

"Leo's here because Collin MacInroy died in the fire yesterday," Mona said.

Aunt Bee took a step back, a wrinkled hand jumping to cover her heart. Her face showed shock, and Mona suddenly regretted blurting out the news. She clutched Aunt Bee's hand and ushered her to the couch.

"Oh, poor Collin! Poor Lacey!" said Aunt Bee. "That's horrible. He was so young."

"Can I get you something to drink?" Mona asked. "I just made a pot of coffee."

Aunt Bee nodded at her, and Mona hesitated for a moment to leave Aunt Bee alone with Leo, but one glance at Leo told her he was back to business. He'd pulled out his notebook and asked Bee, "Did you know Collin very well?"

Mona retreated into the kitchen and poured Aunt Bee a rich sugary cup of coffee. She put a few of Vicki's honey cookies on a small tray and headed back into the living room.

Leo and Aunt Bee dug into the cookies, leaving only crumbs on the tray.

"So, Mona, tell me about the kitchen at *Jammin' Honey*. Did you do any cooking yesterday morning?" Leo asked

Guilt choked Mona, and she couldn't meet Leo's eyes. In her mind, she frantically retraced her steps in the kitchen yesterday. She had turned off the burner. She was sure of it.

She swallowed the lump in her throat and said, "I made a pot of coffee and turned a burner on for a quick batch of jam."

Leo studied her a moment. "Uh huh. Then what?"

"I got a call from Lacey, telling me to get over to the bakery, so I turned the burner off," she hesitated and looked at his face for reassurance. When all she saw was grim determination, she steeled herself and repeated. "I turned the burner off and left the shop."

Leo's fingers drummed on the coffee table. "Are you certain that all sources of heat were turned off?"

"Of course she is!" Aunt Bee screeched.

Mona nodded at Aunt Bee, feeling grateful for her support.

Nothing like a defensive octogenarian in your corner.

"I don't normally leave anything on, maybe the coffee pot since I was coming right back, but that shouldn't have triggered a fire," she answered. "Right, I mean it's got an automatic shutoff ..."

"All the newfangled gadgets have automatic shut offs these days," Aunt Bee said.

Leo nodded. "Right. And the burner, you're sure you turned it off?"

Am I sure?

"Yes, I never leave burners on," Mona said, "At least, I don't normally."

"Never or not normally? To be clear, you don't recall whether you turned off the burner or not, is that correct?"

"Don't badger her!" Aunt Bee squealed.

"I'm not badgering her," Leo said. "I'm asking a clarifying question."

"Ugh! Okay you two, don't argue," Mona exclaimed. "I'm doing the best I can." She buried her head in her hands.

Aunt Bee stood. "Now you've upset her!"

Leo stood too. "I'm sorry. I'm just trying to get to the bottom—"

Mona motioned for them to sit down. "Calm down. I'm sorry to say, I just don't remember exactly. I swear to you, Leo, I really think I turned it off ... but I'm not a 100%."

He nodded and made a note.

What did he just write?

As if reading her mind, Aunt Bee exclaimed, "What did you write down? She turned it off. She says she turned it off! Don't you dare write anything other than that down. I don't care how cute you are!"

Leo smirked. "Okay, Aunt Bee. I don't want to do anything to make you angry."

Mona grabbed at his hand. "Leo, if I left the burner on, it would be the first time I've ever done that."

He gave her a sympathetic look. "Unfortunately, there's a first time for everything, and all it takes is one mistake and you have a mess on your hands," he said.

Mona stiffened.

It's coming out all wrong. I sound like an irresponsible dingbat.

"That morning, can you remember any odors?" Leo asked. "Did you notice smoke or a burning smell?"

"No, not that I can recall, I was in the front of the shop for most of the morning."

"Did you see anything unusual or see anyone acting out of the ordinary in any way?" Leo asked.

Mona racked her brain, every minute of that morning replaying in her mind, "No. I can't say that I noticed anything unusual except for the phone call from Lacey and her insistence that I go to the bakery at once. I asked her if it could wait, and she insisted that it couldn't. You know how Lacey is, she can be …" Mona bit her lip. She remembered Leo had dated Lacey. Maybe he didn't know what she meant at all.

"That Lacey can be pushy," Aunt Bee said.

"Go on," Leo said to Mona.

"I don't mean to suggest anything," Mona said uncomfortably. "Only that she can be demanding at times, at least she can with me."

"Who was at the bakery when you arrived, and is there anyone who can vouch for how long you were there?" Leo asked.

"Vouch for her?" Aunt Bee shrieked. "What do you mean? You can't possibly think Mona had anything to do with that fire or with Collin's death."

Leo looked unfazed, his expression unchanging as Aunt Bee berated him.

Mona tried not to let her annoyance show.

Does he really think I'd lie about being at the bakery?

"Yes, there are people who can *vouch* for me. Lacey and one of her employees," Mona said. "And there were customers at the bakery when I got there, they could confirm my whereabouts."

Lacey can definitely vouch for my whereabouts at the time of the fire, but will she?

Mona twisted the handkerchief Leo had given her, her sorrow slowly turning to anger.

Leo closed his notebook and finished his coffee. "That's it, that's all I need for now. I'll be in touch."

"I bet you will," Aunt Bee murmured.

"Do you have my number?" Mona asked.

"No, let me get that from you," he said.

She gave him her number and absently wondered when he'd call. *Ugh! It feels like high school all over again.*

Leo opened his wallet and handed her a card. "Mona." He glanced at Aunt Bee and cleared his throat. "This is strictly off the record, I talked to the fire chief, and the building isn't a total loss. The fire destroyed the warehouse and the kitchen, and there's some smoke damage to the shop, but the fire department managed to save the shop. Does that help?"

"Will it help her pay back Cecelia?" Aunt Bee asked.

Mona cringed.

"I suppose that will depend on the insurance company and the findings from the arson team." He tapped his notebook, "but my records show you turned off the burner."

"Thank you, Leo," Mona said, as she held herself back from hugging him.

She walked him out the front door and stood on the porch as he drove away.

It's not fair, how he could come home to Magnolia Falls after all those years and climb right back into my heart?

Looking at the mountains, she realized that Leo didn't have to climb back into her heart, he'd never left.

CHAPTER 4

$\mathcal{M}$ona walked back into her house and poured herself and Aunt Bee another cup of coffee.

"A murder," Aunt Bee breathed, clutching the lacy neckline of her blouse. Her eyes sparkled with mischief as she quirked a heavily penciled brow in Mona's direction. "Who do you think done it?"

Mona sighed. "I can't believe you're taking delight in this!"

"Not the murder part," Bee said, doing her best to look offended. "The mystery part! We can help Leo figure this thing out."

"What do you mean we? Leo's a police officer. He doesn't need our help."

"He does so! Anyway, you better insert yourself, if you ever want to get his attention."

It was Mona's turn to be offended. "What do you mean by that?"

Bee patted her hand. "None of us are getting any younger dear. Tick Tock."

"Thanks a lot, Aunt Bee. I know I can always count on you for a shot of confidence!"

"Don't be so sensitive darling. A man like Leo needs a strong woman by his side, and now that Collin is out of the way, it's just a matter of time until that widow gets her hooks into him."

Mona chewed on the inside of her cheek. A part of her knew Aunt Bee was right. "Do you think Collin was the target?" she asked.

Aunt Bee leveled a gaze at her. "Well, I'd rather think it was Collin than you. I can't fathom anyone would want to hurt you!"

A chill crawled up Mona's spine.

Who would want me dead?

Mona sipped the hot coffee, trying to shrug off the growing uneasiness in her gut. "I didn't know Collin was in the warehouse and neither did Vicki, so ..."

"If no one knew he was there, and then whoever set your place on fire was ..." Aunt Bee suddenly looked around the room as if she expected someone to jump through the front window.

"Vicki wasn't in the shop yesterday, so ... was I a target?" Mona asked, sitting heavily down on the couch next to Aunt Bee.

Aunt Bee clucked, "Who's got it out for you girl?"

Mona pressed her fingertips to her forehead and sighed. "I've lived in Magnolia Falls all my life. I never thought anyone was out to get me! I'm not rich and never cheated anyone out of money or messed around with anyone's husband. Who have I made so mad that they'd want to kill me?"

Aunt Bee fiddled with her empty coffee cup and saucer. "Let's see. What about the fellow that owns the Cheese Shop?"

"Alexander Kaas?" Mona asked. "What about him?"

Aunt Bee made a face. "Yeah, him. I never liked him. Do you know he's never given the Coupon Clippers a deal?"

Whether it was nerves or the look on her Aunt's face, Mona collapsed into a fit of giggles.

Her shrill laughter must have frightened Aunt Bee, because she squeaked. "Should I call a doctor?"

Mona collected herself. "No. Sorry. It's just that if I don't laugh, I might cry. You're right, Alexander is at the top of my list of suspects."

Aunt Bee gave her a knowing nod.

"You know, he had quite a markup on my jams and Vicki's honey products. In fact, last summer, if it hadn't been for my blackberry ginger jam and Vicki's honey scented candles, his shop would never have turned a profit."

Aunt Bee stiffened. "Ah ha! The man is going broke without you!"

"Well, I don't know about that, but last summer was tough—"

"So he burns down your shop, and that ends the competition for his store!" Aunt Bee shrieked.

"We weren't really competition though, I mean, we weren't going to sell wine or cheese, it's just that—" Anger flared in Mona's chest as she remembered the day she told Alexander that she was resigning. He told her she was nothing but a dreamer. Told her she would fail, which was why he was happy to forget her resignation and give her a modest raise.

A modest raise, thought Mona.

What a jerk!

A little more money was no incentive for her to stay, and certainly not with his attitude. She'd wanted her freedom and independence.

She sighed.

Be careful what you wish for. Now the shop is gone, and you have no obligations, free as bird, but no closer to your goals.

Mona sipped her coffee, now cold, and said. "Alexander is temperamental, but is he capable of committing a murder or burning down my shop?"

Aunt Bee shrugged. "Who else is mad at you?"

Mona let out a bitter laugh. "Cousin Stewart."

Aunt Bee frowned. "Stewart's angry with you? Why?"

Stewart was Aunt Cecilia's only grandson. There was no doubt in Mona's mind that Stewart was mad at her and had been ever since her Great Aunt Cecilia had loaned her the money for the shop.

Mona bit her lip, but Aunt Bee read her like a book. "What? Is he mad that Cee gave you the money for the shop?"

When Mona only shrugged Aunt Bee shook her head. "What the heck did he want the money for? To fritter it away on girls and booze?"

"I don't know," Mona muttered. "But Stu wouldn't burn down my shop. I'm sure of that."

Aunt Bee looked like she didn't agree, but she pinched her lips together and didn't say another word.

Mona let her mind wander in the silence. She loved to read a good mystery, and she knew that most of the crimes in her favorite novels were motivated by money, as in the case of Alexander or Stewart. The other motivation for murder was love. If the motivation was love, there could be only one person as a potential suspect, Lacey MacInroy.

Lacey made a logical suspect. Leo had come back to town, Lacey was married, but who was to say that she didn't want to be free to pursue Leo once more? The only two people standing in her way were her husband, Collin and her old rival, Mona.

Could Lacey be that cold and clever?

"What about Lacey?" Mona asked out loud.

Aunt Bee smiled, holding up a triumphant finger. "Now that lady knows how to give a discount! Did you know she double stamps the Coupon Clippers membership card every time we buy a donut at her bakery?"

"Oh my lord, Bee. Not everything is about coupons."

"Why not?"

Mona giggled. "Stop it. I mean, what about Lacey as a suspect? You said so yourself, that it was only a matter of time before she had her hooks into Leo. Do you think she could have killed Collin?"

Aunt Bee scratched her head and looked lost in thought. "Hmmm. Her husband Collin is found dead in the warehouse of Jammin' Honey, a mysterious fire killing. And not only killing him and destroying your business, but casting suspicion on you, Mona. Why, it's diabolical and perfect. Killing two birds with one stone."

Mona's stomach churned in anxiety. "Casting suspicion on me? You don't really think anyone's going to believe that I would have set fire to my own store!"

"It was insured, right?" Aunt Bee asked.

Mona covered her face with her hands, suddenly feeling exhausted. "Of course. But the only part of your theory about Lacey that doesn't make sense is why she called me and was so insistent that I come to her bakery right away.

"Maybe she wanted to make sure you were out of the way?" Aunt Bee.

"Right. Because she likes me so much," Mona said, rolling her eyes.

"I don't think Lacey likes anyone," Aunt Bee said.

"She likes you," Mona said.

"She does?"

Mona laughed despite herself. "She gives you double stamps!"

Aunt Bee waved her hand around, annoyed. "That's not because she likes me. It's because she thinks the Coupon Clippers are good for business. Which we are."

"Fair enough. So why did she call me to rush over to the bakery?"

"Maybe she wanted to make sure poor Collin died and no one was there to save him, and if you died in the fire, she couldn't shift the blame to you."

Mona grimaced.

It was all so awful. She hated the thought that someone would have intentionally burned down her shop, especially if that fire was meant to kill Collin.

Yet, Lacey as a suspect made sense.

"The only problem with the Lacey theory is the timing," Mona said. "How could Lacey set the fire and then be back at the bakery in time to meet with me?"

"Did you stop anywhere on the way to the bakery?" Aunt Bee asked.

Mona shook her head. "No, I went directly there."

"Were you chatting on the phone to Vicki or anyone after you parked? Or did you have any trouble finding parking?"

"No, I didn't really delay. I was busy and in a hurry. It did take me a couple minutes to find parking though …"

"That's it!" Aunt Bee declared loudly. "It was her!" She stood and collected her purse.

"What?"

Aunt Bee crossed the living room toward the front door.

Mona jumped off the couch in alarm, trailing her to the front door. "Where are you going?" Mona asked, imagining her Great Aunt rushing over to police headquarters and demanding to speak Leo.

"It's almost 10 O'clock. I have to facilitate our Coupon Clipper meeting at the library. "You should come."

Relief swept over Mona. She didn't have the strength to rein in her Aunt if she got into a stubborn streak about Leo.

Mona opened the door for her Aunt. "No, thanks Aunt Bee. I think I need to lay low and lick my wounds."

Aunt Bee pressed her cheek to Mona's. "Don't let 'em keep you down too long darling. The world needs you."

Mona watched as Aunt Bee shuffled off her porch and settled herself into her behemoth rusting Cadillac. She waved as the Cadillac slowly rolled out of sight. She couldn't believe her aunt actually encouraged her this time.

Mona's house sat back from the main road on a large piece of property surrounded by trees. Her nearest neighbor was over a quarter of a mile down the mountain. She always found solace in the privacy of her home, but now a dreaded thought snaked into her brain.

If anything happens to me, if I scream for help, no one will hear me.

If someone is trying to kill me, I'm way more vulnerable at home where there are no witnesses.

She gazed out at the oak trees surrounding her. The bucolic country setting always settled her mind and soothed her nerves, but not this time. Feeling vulnerable, Mona's senses heightened, every noise in the forest sounding ominous.

A sense of dread overwhelmed her.

She rushed back inside the house. Her hands trembled as she locked the front door.

Anxiety bubbled in her belly, and for the first time Mona could remember, she didn't want to be by herself; she was afraid.

Should I call Vicki to come stay with me? Mona thought.

But then she could be putting Vicki in danger.

I should call Leo!

And what would she tell him? She didn't have one shred of evidence against Alexander, Stewart, or Lacey.

A surge of determination bolstered her. She had fought long and hard for her dream to open the shop. She wasn't going to let anyone take it away from her, not her old boss, not her jealous cousin and certainly not Prom Queen Lacey. She wouldn't let a fire stop her.

"I'm going to find the culprit," Mona said to herself through gritted teeth.

Or ... what?

Die trying? She shivered at the thought.

CHAPTER 5

 he phone in Mona's kitchen rang jolting her out of her Miss Marple reverie. She shook her head and raced for the phone.

Who could be calling me on my landline?

It seemed no one ever called that number anymore. Everyone she knew always dialed her cell.

She answered the phone with a careful, "Hello."

"Mona, I hope I haven't caught you at a bad time?" asked a voice on the other end of the line that Mona immediately recognized.

"Mrs. Fletcher," Mona considered lying to the woman, but she detested lying, and so she gritted her teeth and answered truthfully, "No, I'm not busy, I've a few minutes, how are you?"

"I'm fine, my dear I just wanted to call you and tell you not to worry, there are people like me in this town, that don't believe a word of it, not a word."

Mona was confused by Mrs. Fletcher's response, "Mrs. Fletcher, I'm not sure I know what you mean."

"You don't have to be strong with me, you can cry all you want. I won't tell a soul."

A bad feeling oozed into Mona's gut. "Um. I'm still not sure what you are talking about."

"If that is how you are coping at this terrible time, I understand, but I don't believe a word of it, all that talk about arson and insurance money, it's just terrible."

Mona slowly sat down on a kitchen chair, "Arson?" she managed to ask in a squeaky voice.

How in the world has word traveled so fast?

"You are a brave one, putting on a front, but it's alright, I know you would never have left the burner on or did anything to start a fire for a huge insurance check, not you."

The tone of Mrs. Fletcher's voice gave Mona the impression that the woman was pandering to her, trying to find out information that could be used as currency among the other town gossips.

Mona swallowed her rising nausea and said, "Mrs. Fletcher, I'm lucky to have a friend as faithful as you, you implied earlier that everyone was talking about this, does everyone think I'm an arsonist?"

"I'm sorry to have upset you and I can't speak for everyone ... but many people think ..." her voice hitched down a notch and she practically whispered, "They think you're guilty of setting the fire. But you know how misguided people can be. I would *never* suspect you of committing such an act. Unless, of course, you were due to get back a real big insurance payout. Then well, who could blame you. Did you have the place insured for a lot of money?"

Mona held the phone away from her ear for a moment, she couldn't believe the nerve of this woman. Was she really asking, how much money *Jammin' Honey* was insured for, it was inconceivable.

Taking a deep breath, Mona said, "Mrs. Fletcher, I'm sorry to disappoint you, but I absolutely did *not* set fire to my own shop. I would never do that, no matter how much insurance money."

"Oh dear, I've upset you. I certainly didn't mean to suggest—"

"Yes, you did!" Mona said, irritated with herself for taking the bait.

"Now, no need to upset yourself. Listen, dear, I've got a casserole I need to prepare—"

"Well, just a minute, Mrs. Fletcher," Mona said, biting back her frustration. After all, maybe there was a use for gossips. "Did you know that Collin MacInroy was killed in the fire?"

Mrs. Fletcher let out an exaggerated gust of breath. "I did hear that. Yes, dear. What a shame. A real shame."

"Um hum," Mona agreed. "Well, Mrs. Fletcher, do you know anything about Colin and Lacey?"

Silence greeted Mona and for a moment she thought the line had disconnected. She stared down at the phone and remembered it was a landline. "Mrs. Fletcher?"

"Yes dear."

"Did you hear my question?"

"Yes dear."

"Uh ... well, do you know anything about Collin and Lacey?"

"Like what exactly would you like to know?"

Like did Lacey murder her husband! Mona wanted to scream, but instead she asked.

"For example, do you know why Collin was in my warehouse?"

Again, the woman didn't immediately answer, and Mona wondered whether the woman was hard of hearing or just stunned into silence.

"Mrs. Fletcher, are you still there? Mrs. Fletcher?"

Mona could hear the woman breathing so she waited for her to answer.

Finally, Mrs., Fletcher spoke, "Mona, my dear, I hear you, I'm just trying to think about how to tell you this. It's not very nice and I don't want to be the one to have to tell you, but ..."

Mona knew that the woman was baiting her like a fish, drawing her in with a teasing phrase, a masterful technique of a professional gossip. Mona had no other choice but to bite, "It's okay, after the disaster I've had, it can't get any worse, go ahead and tell me."

"If you insist, now I'm just telling you what I heard, you know that I don't believe it."

"Yes, of course you don't believe it," said Mona, as she tried to be convincing as she lied to the woman, "Please, tell me."

"Alright, I can't say for sure why Collin was in the warehouse, but there is a rumor around town that you and he may have had something going on, that maybe he was in the warehouse because that is where you two, you know I don't like to say, but had your rendezvous."

Mona nearly dropped the phone at the idea that she would ever be a home wrecker; she was appalled at the suggestion, "What? You must be kidding? I've never run around with a married man in my life!"

"I know dear, you are a good girl, but you know how people can be. It's no secret that Lacey and Collin weren't happy. Folks say he had a wandering eye, first with that Stephanie Tyndall and then you."

Stephanie Tyndall?

Mona had never heard that rumor. She knew Stephanie had worked at Lacey's bakery, and rumor was that she'd been fired. But Mona thought they said Lacey claimed the till was short ... not that Stephanie had been fooling around with Collin.

I'm so out of the gossip loop, Mona thought with little regret.

"I know that can't be true because," Mrs. Fletcher droned on. "No offense, but Lacey is so young and pretty, just like a woman you see on TV, why would a man ever run around on a woman like that with Stephanie Tyndall of all people and no offense, you? You are a sweet girl but to be honest, you aren't exactly a beauty, not like Lacey."

Heat rose to Mona's cheeks; she wasn't sure what was more upsetting, that people around town thought she was Collin's mistress or that Mrs. Fletcher just insulted her.

Trying to maintain her composure and control of the conversation, she asked Mrs. Fletcher about Collin and Lacey's marital problems, "Mrs. Fletcher, you said they weren't happy, what do you know about that?"

"A lady I know from church used to clean house for them. She told me once that they argued and fought a lot, she didn't know about what exactly, but I always figured it was because poor dear Lacey thought he ran around on her."

"What if he didn't run around on her? What if Lacey was trying to get out of the marriage? Maybe she was unhappy, could that have been why they were arguing?"

"Maybe so, I never thought of it like that, I mean Lacey is such a dear, sweet girl, and she loved her husband. She stuck by him even after the rumors went around about his affair with Stephanie Tyndall. I always thought the problem was him."

Mona's stomach tightened, threatening to heave up this morning's coffee if she listened to one more minute of Mrs. Fletcher singing Lacey's praises, "Mrs. Fletcher, you've been very helpful. Thank you for being a friend during my time of trouble, and I appreciate that you were honest with me about what folks are saying. I'll let you get back to your casserole."

"Mona, honey, it was good talking to you, call me anytime you need a friend. You know I'm here for you."

Mona's fist clenched as she said through gritted teeth, "I sure will. Good bye," she hung up the phone and screamed in frustration.

Sitting at the table in her kitchen, she realized that not only did the town think she was an arsonist, but Collin's mistress.

Could Lacey have dreamed up the whole scheme to get rid of her husband and me, but why did she call me?

Mona's instinct told her that Lacey was somehow at the center of her present woes. Thinking about Mrs. Fletcher's description of Lacey as a sweet girl, the victim of an unhappy marriage to an adulterous husband, she wondered if Lacey was responsible for the rumors about her and Stephanie, trying to garner public sympathy. Knowing Lacey, Mona would not put it past her, even the murder of her husband.

I have to talk to Stephanie.

Mona cleared the cups and saucers from Leo and Aunt Bee's visit to the sink. Suddenly the realization that Leo was investigating hit her hard.

Oh No!

What if Leo hears these rumors and thinks I had an affair with Collin?

CHAPTER 6

*A*s Mona did the dishes, her mind wandered to Leo. She wanted to call him, but what would she say?

"Hey, I talked to the local gossip, and just so you know, I wasn't having an affair with Collin, because, you know, I'd never do that. I'm in love with you."

In her frustration, a water glass slipped from her soapy hand and crashed against her tile floor, splintering into a million pieces.

Ugh!

She stooped to pick up the largest piece and sliced her hand on the rim. Blood dripped from her fingers and she grabbed the broom and cleaned the mess.

I need to get out of the house. I'm a nervous wreck!

After bandaging her hand, she grabbed her purse and headed to her car. There was only one place she knew for certain she'd find comfort.

She drove directly to Vicki's farm. The winding road and the sound of the wind in the pines, soothed her as she drove. It was a quick 10-minute drive, but it gave her time to sort her thoughts.

Top suspect: Lacey.

Although she wasn't about to let Alexander Kaas or Cousin Stu off the hook yet. And she probably needed to make time to talk to Stephanie.

Mona pulled onto Vicki's private road and was a bit annoyed to see another car next to Vicki's pickup truck. It was a non-descript blue sedan.

Oh no!

What kind of car was Leo driving these days?

Please Lord! Tell me Leo's not here.

She wasn't ready to face him yet. Not if he was in the know about the rumors. What would she say to him?

She was about to turn her car around when Vicki stepped out onto the porch with a pitcher of lemonade. With her free hand she waved to Mona.

With her belly full of dread, Mona put the car in park. Then before she could get overly stressed about seeing Leo, Alexander Kaas stepped out on the porch next to Vicki.

Alexander? What the in the world is he doing here?

The moment she caught sight of his smug face, she knew.

He's here to talk Vicki back into selling honey at his shop!

Alexander stood on the porch, his long blond hair swirling in the wind, and his arms crossed. He wore a tight white t-shirt with a black leather vest over it, and Mona was sure he'd crossed his arms for the sole purpose of flexing his massive biceps at her.

She wasn't impressed but could swear she saw Vicki practically swoon.

She stepped out of her car and headed toward the porch.

"Howdy!" Vicki called excitedly.

"Hey," Mona grumbled.

"What happened to your hand?" Vicki asked.

Mona waved away her concern. "Nothing. Just clumsy.

"Mona," Alexander said, a solemn expression on his face. "I'm so sorry about *Jammin' Honey*. I know how much opening the store meant to you."

Mona took in his words and bit her lip. She knew he could be phony and petty, but why pick a fight?

"Thank you, Alexander."

Vicki motioned to her porch swing. "Take a load off, honey. You want some lemonade?" Vicki glanced nervously at Alexander and Mona had the distinct impression that she was interrupting something.

Alexander cleared his throat and said, "Uh. Let me get the glasses." He spun around and retreated into the house.

Mona urgently grabbed Vicki's hand and whispered. "What's he doing here?"

Vicki shrugged defensively. "What do you mean? He came by to see how I'm holding up. It was my store too, you know."

"I know. I know. I'm sorry. *Jammin' Honey* was every bit as much yours as it was mine," Mona said, regretting her harsh tone.

It was true that it'd been Mona's Great Aunt Cecilia who loaned them the seed money, but Mona and Vicki were 50/50 partners.

"I think it was sweet of him," Vicki said, her face beaming.

Oh Lord. She's practically glowing!

"Vicki! You can't fall for a guy like that!"

"Like what?" Vicki said. "He's always been uber nice to me. Plus, he's hot!"

"He could be a criminal!" Mona hissed.

"What? Oh, come on! You can't think Alexander had anything to do with the fire!"

"Why not?"

Vicki shrugged helplessly. "Why would he? Come on, Mona, this is Alexander we're talking about. We worked with him for a year!"

"His shop was losing money before we started selling our products there!"

Vicki's front door popped open, and Alexander appeared with a pink and yellow tray filled with glasses and Vicki's trade-mark strawberry and honey thumbprint cookies.

Mona bit her lip. She knew she couldn't talk to Vicki about the fire or any more of her suspicions with Alexander present. "Oh, so sorry. I need to go." She leaned in for a quick hug from Vicki and said, "I'll call you later."

Vicki flashed her a sad smile, and Mona squeezed her hand.

"Don't worry about it," Mona said. "We'll figure everything out later." She rushed off the porch to her car and called over her shoulder, "Have fun, you two!"

She quickly backed down the private road and sped toward Antioch Avenue. She remembered that Stephanie Tyndall's family lived on that road. She didn't know if Stephanie still lived there, but it was as good a place as any to start, and right now she needed answers.

Racking her brain, she thought about what she knew about Stephanie. She knew Stephanie used to work at the bakery until Lacey one day blew a gasket and fired her.

Mona never paid much attention to the rumor mill. She'd always thought there was accusation of a money shortage at the bakery when Stephanie worked there, but could it be true that Stephanie and Collin had some sort of affair?

How exactly am I supposed to ask Stephanie about that?

Well, even if Stephanie had never crossed the line with Collin, she may still have inside information into the relationship between Lacey and her husband.

It's worth a try.

From inside her purse, Mona's cell phone buzzed. She rummaged around and glanced at the caller I.D. Cousin Stewart. Feeling only marginally guilty, Mona put him into her voicemail.

I'll deal with him later, she promised herself.

Mona turned off Antioch Avenue and onto a smaller dirt road. The Tyndalls had lived in the same valley for generations; there was a creek, a campground for tourists, and rental property. The family occupied a few small houses set back from the road. Mona drove up the narrow, dirt road and hoped that the Tyndall family would be welcoming.

Slowly making her way up the narrow driveway, she put the car in park behind a rusty Ford truck. She honked the horn to announce her arrival. Two hunting dogs climbed out from under the porch and met her at the car. A man came to the door of the house and called out to the dogs who quickly returned to the porch.

Mona opened the car door and spoke to him, "Sir, I'm Mona Reilly, I was looking for Stephanie Tyndall's house."

The man looked at her for a long time without saying a word, then he spoke, "I know who you are, Stephanie's house is up the road a ways, about a quarter mile."

Anxiety churned in Mona's chest. She didn't like the way the man had looked at her.

Whatever happened to innocent until proven guilty?

Mona dug deep and flashed him her most endearing smile and said, "Thank you, sir."

She climbed back in her car and followed his directions that led to a small house set high on a ridge that overlooked the valley. Mona honked the horn once more and waited.

I hope Stephanie is a little more welcoming then her neighbors!

A woman walked out onto the porch, and Mona was relieved that it was Stephanie.

"Hi Mona! What brings you to our side of the mountain?"

"I was hoping you'd have time for a quick chat."

"Sure, come on," Stephanie said. She motioned for Mona to sit on an old-fashioned gliding rocking chair nestled in the corner of the porch. "I've just made a hot pot of green tea. Can I offer you some?"

"That would be lovely," Mona said.

When Stephanie went inside, Mona fidgeted on the porch. The view was breathtaking, and in the distance, the sound of a waterfall trickling soothed Mona.

What am I going to say to her?

Stephanie returned with a tray of tea and finger sandwiches. Mona realized with sudden surprise that she was famished. She crunched on a cucumber sandwich and grinned at Stephanie.

"Goodness, this is the best sandwich I've had in a long time!"

Stephanie laughed. "I'm glad you like it. I baked the bread myself."

"It's delicious."

"Thank you. Its gluten-free, but I don't normally tell people that until after they've tried it."

Mona laughed. "Why? You think people are against gluten-free?"

Stephanie shrugged. "Lacey sure is."

Mona stiffened. "Really?"

Stephanie tilted her head. "Did you come all this way to talk about gluten?"

Mona smiled. "Honestly, Stephanie, I don't know if you heard about my shop—"

Stephanie nodded sadly. "I did see something about the fire on the news last night. Mona. I'm so sorry."

"Thank you," Mona paused, then decided it was probably best to get straight to the point. "Stephanie, I know we don't know each other very well, but I could use your help."

Stephanie seemed surprised. "Sure! With what?"

"Colin MacInroy was in my warehouse at the time of the fire—"

Stephanie gasped, and a hand flew to cover her mouth. "Oh no! Is he okay?"

"I'm afraid not," Mona said, fighting a lump in her throat at the other woman's reaction. "He perished."

Stephanie dropped her head at the news and looked visibly shaken. "He's dead? Are you certain?"

Mona nodded stiffly. She hadn't been prepared for an emotional reaction and awkwardly hugged the woman. "I'm so sorry, Stephanie. Were you and Collin close?"

Oh lord. If the rumors are true, I've just told her that her lover is dead. What am I doing? I'm in way over my head.

Stephanie wiggled out of Mona's arms and wiped her tear-streaked cheeks. "No, we weren't exceptionally close. It's just that I … he was a sweet guy." The look on Stephanie's face changed as she studied Mona. "Oh. I see what you mean. Goodness. I hope you haven't bought into any of the awful gossip around town. Collin and I were never more than friends, and really only acquaintances at that."

"Stephanie, I'm sorry, I didn't mean to imply—"

"I know you didn't, it just that those awful rumors about Collin and me cost me my job. Now what can I do for you? I can't say that I can be much help."

"That's just it, you may be able to help me more than anyone. I don't mean to pry, but I need to know about Collin."

The other woman's eyes narrowed, and her expression turned grave, "Like I said, we were only acquaintances, what would I know about Collin?"

"You worked at the bakery for many years and ... I just thought ... I'm sorry. I really don't mean any offense."

"It's okay. None taken, it's just a sore subject with me. I haven't been able to shake those awful rumors since they started. And then just when people started to believe me, Lacey started another lie about my stealing from the till. Can you imagine?"

Mona shifted nervously, too mortified to say that she'd heard that rumor.

"Anyway, I haven't exactly been straight with you. Collin and I were friends. Not lovers, but more than acquaintances. Mostly because we had a few things in common, we had our troubles."

"What do you mean?"

"I mean, my brother, Gabe committed suicide when he came back from Afghanistan. He suffered from PTSD; I tried to help him, to support him, but he was too proud to ask for help or accept it. He shot himself with our Grandfather's shotgun down in that valley just below."

Mona's eyes involuntarily left Stephanie's face and gazed down into the valley; it was a peaceful place, and it was hard to imagine such a horrible scene playing out there.

"Stephanie, I'm so sorry for your loss, I had no idea."

"It's alright; I can talk about it now. Like I was saying, I couldn't save my brother, but I wasn't going to let another soldier die the same way, and Collin was my chance to redeem myself and save a life."

"Are you saying that he suffered from the same ailment, PTSD?"

"Yes ma'am. Collin had it bad, poor guy. His wife, little miss Barbie doll didn't care about him when he was down and couldn't get back up. All she wanted was Collin to be happy and to take care of her, hell, he couldn't even take care of himself most times."

"Stephanie, was that where the problem started, with Lacey?"

"Probably, his illness was why he and I became friends. We understood each other, I looked out for him and gave him a shoulder to lean on, and he let me try to save him. He knew about Gabe, and he helped me understand the pain my brother was going through before he died. If it wasn't for Collin, I would never have been able to forgive myself."

"You know, Collin died in my warehouse, do you have any idea why he may have been there?"

Stephanie sighed. "I think I know why he was there. I don't like to talk about their personal life, but I suppose you are just as involved as I am, a victim of it same as me. Lacey was unhappy with Collin; she was looking for a way out if you ask me."

"Do you mean she wanted a divorce?"

"I think so, I can't say for sure. His PTSD would flare up sometimes, and it was more than he or she could handle. See, you have to understand something, Collin loved Lacey, and he tried to be strong for her, but Lacey didn't want to have to put up with him when he was broken and needed help."

"That sounds right, like the Lacey I know, but about the warehouse?"

"He would have episodes, really bad ones. He was ashamed of it and didn't want anyone to know. At first, he'd come up here. Stay in my spare bedroom ... but when the rumors started, he didn't want to come here anymore. Didn't want to cause trouble for me. I didn't know he was in your warehouse, but that makes sense now. He'd have done anything to hide his demons from Lacey. He didn't want her to know just how bad it really was for him. So, he'd hole up somewhere that he wouldn't be disturbed. Sounds like your warehouse fit the bill. He could go there and not have to be strong for anyone, he could fight his demons, cry, do what he needed to and go back to Lacey like nothing ever happened."

"That poor man," said Mona.

Stephanie let out a long breath. "Don't you feel sorry for him, there's nothing poor about him. His pain is over, he is in a far better place. Maybe now he can find peace."

CHAPTER 7

*M*ona left Stephanie's house with a heavy heart. The conversation had been an eye-opening experience for Mona. PTSD wasn't a subject she understood or knew much about until she spoke with Stephanie. Mona was struck by Stephanie's honesty and willingness to discuss the condition that had caused her brother to take his own life and drove Collin into hiding in dark, unknown places like her warehouse.

Driving down the mountain, she stopped her car briefly in the valley and said a quick prayer for Stephanie's departed brother, Gabe. Despite the warm weather, she felt a chill crawl up her spine as she drove back home.

Gabe had killed himself...

An ominous thought nagged at the back of Mona's head.

Could Collin have done the same...

Maybe it was Collin that started the fire?

Maybe he was looking for a way to end everything ... but why burn down her shop in the process?

Mona made her way home with morbid thoughts swirling in her head. She contemplated going to see Lacey but thought better of it. Maybe she needed to leave the investigation up to the police.

She pulled onto her own private road, ready to call it a day, when her cell phone buzzed in her purse. She took it out and saw it was Aunt Bee.

"Hello Honey," Aunt Bee said cheerfully. "I'm just checking in to make sure you're not sulking too much."

Mona smiled despite herself. "Not too much."

"Good, good. We can't let material losses get us down. Everything will work out in the end. You'll see."

"Thanks Aunt Bee," Mona said, climbing out of the car and making her way to her front door.

She was ready to end the call when Bee said, "Hang on! I have good news."

"Great. I need some of that."

"The Coupon Clippers are super excited about your BOGO."

"What?"

"The BOGO on your special blackberry ginger jam."

Mona paused at her front door. "Um ... I don't think I can do that anymore Aunt Bee—"

"Nonsense! It's exactly what you need to do. It will keep you busy and bring in a little cash flow for you dear."

"Bee, it's not like I'm hurting for cash so much that a few jars of jam—"

"Well then it's settled!"

"What? No, I—"

"And it's not just a few jars mind you. You remember Alana? She runs that blog *Frugalicious*. She's going to feature you. Said she get gets over a hundred thousand views a day. You could really move some products!"

With her free hand, Mona dug around in her purse and pulled out her house keys. She was fighting overwhelm as she said, "I suppose that's a good opportunity, but how many jars—"

"Not jars, darling," Aunt Bee cooed. "Cases!"

Mona stuck her key in the door and stopped cold. "Oh no."

"What?" Aunt Bee asked. "I think preparing the jam in your kitchen will be the perfect antidote to keep you busy. You've always told—"

"My door is unlocked!" Mona whispered into the phone.

"What's that dear?"

"I could have sworn I locked my door when I left."

"Oh, don't worry too much, darling. That happens to me all the time," Aunt Bee said.

But Mona couldn't help herself, her heart thudded in her chest, and her palms grew slick with moisture. "I … let me call you later, Aunt Bee."

Anger flared inside Mona. She would not be a victim! She would not allow someone to break into her home while she cowered. Without thinking, Mona kicked it into overdrive. She pushed open her front door and called out, "Hello?"

She tore through her house, dashing from one room to another, screaming out, "Is someone here? Hello?"

There was no response to her calls, in fact, the house was deathly silent.

She examined each room, more slowly and realized nothing seemed out of place.

Oh Lord, I'm losing my mind!

Did I really leave my front door unlocked?

She returned to her front porch and looked outside. There were no other car treads on her dirt driveway except the ones from her own car.

I'm getting completely paranoid, she thought.

The sound of frogs and crickets singing their sunset opera, should have soothed her, but instead it made her antsy. The day had evaporated, and she was no closer to finding out who had set fire to her dreams.

The thought made her blood pressure rise. She needed answers.

It was embarrassing to admit, but she had already memorized Leo's number from the card he gave her at their morning meeting; she dialed his number and prayed he would answer.

"Detective Lawson."

"Hi, Leo, It's Mona, do you have a second?"

"Sure I do, what's going on? How are you holding up?"

A rush of warmth heated Mona, and she almost felt giddy.

He cares how I'm holding up!

"I'm alright. I had an upsetting phone call after you left, I don't want to say from who, but it was troubling, and I need to ask you something," Mona answered.

"Ask me anything."

"I feel silly, really. But it came to my attention that there's an awful rumor flying around town that Collin and I ..." She hesitated and cleared her throat. "Some people think that Collin and I were having an affair. And I wanted to make sure you knew ... well ... that the police, you know ... that the record show ..."

Oh lord, I'm making an idiot of myself!

"I wasn't having an affair with Collin, Leo. I want to be clear about that. I hardly knew him. And we certainly weren't having an affair."

The silence on the phone was deafening. "Leo, are you still there?"

"I'm still here, Mona, I was hoping you wouldn't hear anything about that, I'm furious that the information leaked. You know how small towns can be. I'm not supposed to discuss it with you, but since you know about it anyway, I suppose it won't hurt."

Mona could feel the beginning of an anxiety attack, she tried to steady herself and asked, "Leo, you think it's true? You can't believe that I would actually have an affair with a married man?"

"It doesn't matter what I believe, I have to investigate the case from all angles and consider every possibility. A case like this would be bad enough if it was just arson but with the murder of a well-known citizen, I have to research every theory, regardless of my own feelings."

"This is horrible, you know I'm not capable of anything like that," said Mona.

"I hate to ask this right now with you being upset, but I'm going to need for you to come down to the station tomorrow."

Her heart racing, she asked quietly, "Are you going to arrest me?"

"No, I'm not going to arrest you. I just have a few more questions that's all. Look, don't let any rumors get to you, it's just part of the investigation, nothing more."

"Alright, thanks Leo. I'll see you tomorrow, what time?"

"How about the morning, around ten?"

"I'll be there. Good bye," she said, her hands shaking as she hung up.

He can't really believe I had anything to do with the fire.

What are they saying now? That I was mad at my lover and burned down my own shop?

She took a deep breath and tried to calm down. She admired the red color of the setting sun and told herself everything would work out.

In her head, she replayed every piece of the conversation with Leo. He had said not to worry about the arson charges. He was trying to soothe her frazzled nerves. It made her want him even more. He was a good man.

And she'd be seeing him in the morning. Now that was something to look forward to.

She returned inside the house and was dreaming about him before her head hit the pillow.

Now only one question loomed.

What do I wear tomorrow?

CHAPTER 8

The next morning, Mona was in surprisingly good spirits for a woman who was going to the police station to answer questions. Especially about a fire where she was the suspected arsonist. She sang in the shower and thought about how handsome Leo was and how sweet he had been during this ordeal.

As she dressed in a crisp pair of khakis and a button down blue shirt, she wrestled with her own heart. She promised herself that after he broke her heart in high school she'd never allow herself to fall in love with him again. Selecting the perfect earrings and necklace, she realized that she was breaking that promise to herself.

But high school was so long ago.

Everyone deserves a second chance.

The drive into town was pleasant, and Mona sang along to the satellite radio in her car. She turned to a station that specialized in sappy love songs and sang along with each one. Catching a glimpse of herself in the rear-view mirror, she looked crazy. A killer was probably on the loose, her shop burned down, and she was dreaming about the handsome detective.

She arrived at the police station, parked her car and walked inside.

After a quick exchange with the receptionist, she waited patiently in the lobby for Leo to arrive. Holding up her cell phone, she took one last look at her hair and make-up, double checking for any flaws. Every hair was in place and her make-up had not smeared, she was pleased with her image and turned the phone off.

"Miss Reilly, I'm glad you could make it, please come with me," said Leo as he coolly greeted her and escorted her to his office.

He's so formal! Mona thought, worriedly following him through a labyrinth of corridors and desks to a small office.

He invited her to have a seat, saying, "I'll be with you in just a second. I promise." He left the room, leaving Mona alone for a moment in his office.

Mona looked around the room and took a deep breath, the scent of his cologne, clean and masculine, hung in the air. Her mind drifted to wondering what time he was off, and if he had any dinner plans, when suddenly she was brought back to the present by the sound of his voice.

Just outside his office door, which was left ajar, she heard him speaking in a quiet voice to another man. Mona strained to listen to the conversation as it seemed to pertain to her and to the case.

"Lawson," said the other man in a low tone, "I know I don't have to say this, but it's important; this case involves your sister and this woman, Mona Reilly that you have known for years, do I have your assurance there is no conflict of interest?"

"Chief, I don't know what to say, what would give you the impression there is a conflict of interest?" asked Leo.

"Isn't Mona your sister's business partner and the woman that owned the shop? Can you honestly tell me that you can remain impartial? If you cannot, I don't want to jeopardize this case, just tell me, and I can assign it to another officer."

"Sir, there is no conflict of interest, absolutely none. Mona really is a friend and business partner of my sister, but she doesn't mean anything to me. I hope that puts this to rest."

"It does, so no feelings there, not an old high school flame, eh Lawson?"

"Not a chance, sir."

Mona sat motionless in the chair, afraid to move, to breathe, to do anything. Leo had told the Chief of police that there wasn't a thing between them, nothing.

She doesn't mean anything to me.

Those words repeated in her head as she felt a familiar feeling, the feeling of her heart being broken all over again by Leo. She immediately recalled when Leo took Lacey to the prom. Mona remembered it all like it was yesterday, the feelings of betrayal and anguish.

In an instant, Mona's memory drifted back to that terrible summer that Mona and Leo spent nearly every day in each other's company. They were as close as best friends, and there seemed to be a mutual attraction between them. Without saying a word to her, Leo suddenly stopped calling her and coming to her house. It was Vicki that told her why, that he was dating Lacey, beautiful, popular Lacey the cheerleader, the homecoming queen, everything Mona wasn't.

That desperate feeling of uncontrollable sadness and loss descended on Mona as she sat in his office. Watching the door, she dreaded it opening, of seeing him walk in. All she wanted was to curl up and die, but she knew that wasn't an option. *I was so stupid to think anything could change between us!*

She remembered Mrs. Fletcher praising Lacey's beauty and felt like she wanted to punch a hole in the wall. A noise behind her sounded as if Leo was about to enter the room, so she straightened in the chair and smoothed down her shirt.

"Hey, sorry about that," Leo said, coming into the room. "Do you want some coffee or something?" he asked.

"I'm fine," Mona said in a stilted voice that she barely recognized as her own.

He quirked an eyebrow at her but said nothing. He sat down at the desk and ran his hand through his hair. He sighed and reached for a file in the top drawer of his desk. He opened the file and turned to Mona. From his furrowed brow and frown, she could see that he was stressed.

Part of her wanted to reach out to him, to take care of him but the other part of her could barely look at him. Each time her gaze fell on his face, she was terrified she would say or do something stupid, like burst into some uncontrollable emotion.

Leo drummed his fingertips on his desk. "So...uh...you and Collin ..."

Mona leveled a gaze. "We were not having an affair."

"Right," Leo said.

Is it my imagination or does he look relieved?

"Apparently, he was suffering from PTSD. That's why he was in my warehouse."

Leo frowned. "Yeah. I know about the PTSD. We served together in Afghanistan until he got discharged a couple years ago ... But how do you know about it?"

Mona shifted uncomfortably in her in chair. "I talked to Stephanie Tyndall yesterday."

Leo's eyes darkened. "I didn't know you and Stephanie were friends."

"We're not."

Confusion clouded Leo's handsome face. "I don't understand. Why did you talk to her then?"

"I wanted to find out what Collin was doing in my warehouse—"

"Whoa, whoa. You have to leave the investigating up to the police."

"Someone burned down my shop, Leo. I can't sit around doing nothing."

"I'm not asking you to do nothing! I'm asking you to leave the investigation to me." He stared at her.

"I have a list of people," she muttered.

"What?" he asked.

She reddened. "Suspects, you know."

He motioned for her to spit it out, and she rushed to share her theory about Alexander. "He was at Vicki's yesterday trying to get her to sell her honey at his shop again."

Leo nodded. "I know, but that doesn't prove he set fire to your place."

60

"My cousin Stewart is mad at me and he could have set the place up, just to ..."

"Just to what? Punish you?"

As if eavesdropping on her conversation, a text from Stewart suddenly appeared on her phone: *ARE YOU AVOIDING ME?*

Mona swiped right on her phone, dismissing the text before Leo could see it.

She sighed. All her theories were sounding hollow and silly in front of Leo. She shrugged. "I don't know. What if Collin wanted to kill himself and burned the placed down?"

Leo frowned. "Go out in a blaze of fury?"

"Stephanie's brother, Gabe, had PTSD. He shot himself."

Leo glanced at the open file on his desk. "I doubt Collin set the place on fire, based on the location of where his body was recovered, but I'll share that theory with the coroner."

Mona sighed. "And then there's Lacey ..."

"What about her? You think she set fire to your place? Why would she do that?"

"What if she was trying to get Collin out of the way?"

Leo shook his head. "She didn't know Collin was at the warehouse. He hadn't been home in days. She thought he was with Stephanie Tyndall. Figured he'd left her."

Mona felt sick to her stomach. All her theories were going up in smoke faster than her shop had.

Leo began a slew of questions surrounding timing, movement, whereabouts, technical questions about the store, the burner, the kitchen, her phone calls and schedules. She answered as best she could, but the details were a blur. She had the distinct impression that Leo was trying to prove that the fire wasn't her fault.

But had it been?

An excruciating hour later, she found herself sitting in the driver's seat of her car. She didn't remember walking out of the police station or saying good bye to Leo.

How did my life take such a quick turn into nowheresvillle?

Looking at her steering wheel and her keys in her hand, she wasn't sure what to do. If she'd left that darn burner on, she'd never get the insurance money. Worse, if she'd left it on, she'd killed an innocent man.

Tears fell from her eyes, and her breathing was ragged as she began to cry. Mona was vaguely aware that her body was shaking as she sat in her car, weeping.

She cried until she was unable to weep one more tear. Heaving, she tried to catch her breath as she wiped her face with her hand.

Sitting in the parking lot of the police station, Mona was at her wit's end.

She put the car in drive and without thinking about it, drove to the shop and parked the car across the street from the burnt remains of her dream. A compulsion to come here was the best explanation she had for why she ended up looking at evidence of the train wreck her life had become.

She got out of the car and walked to the shop, or what was left of it.

She closed her eyes and in her mind, visualized the morning of the fire. She mentally retraced her steps and now standing in front of the charred remains, she was more certain than ever before.

I turned that darn burner off. I know I did.

I'm innocent.

She looked at the wreckage with a critical eye. The kitchen and the warehouse seemed to be the most affected part of the shop. The blaze left them in shambles, but the front of the store was in relatively good condition.

Police tape kept her from venturing into the shop, or else she would have walked into the ashes and began cleaning up the debris. It was astonishing to Mona to think that with a little capital and some hard work, the shop could be rebuilt.

Am I crazy? Could I rebuild this shop?

As Mona stared at the shop and imagined it the way it was just before the fire, she felt a small flicker of hope. She didn't have anything left that was true, Leo would probably never love her, someone in Magnolia Falls wanted her to fail, and the town thought she was an arsonist, but this shop was her dream and she refused to give it up.

Desperately in need of cheering up, she returned to her car and drove to see the one person she could depend on, Vicki. She arrived at Vicki's farm to find her best friend chopping weeds in the garden in the hot sun.

"You need some help?" asked Mona.

Vicki stood up, leaned against the hoe and surveyed Mona, "You are dressed too fancy to get dirty in this garden with me, let me finish this row of carrots and I'll join you on the porch."

"Sounds like a deal. Is the door unlocked? I'll make something to drink."

"Should be, there's lemonade in the fridge and a pitcher of ice tea. And pull out the mini pot pies from the oven. They should be about done. They're gluten-free. I was making them for you."

Mona smiled as she left Vicki and opened the door of the farm-house. The wood floors creaked as she walked across them. The house was over a hundred years old, and Mona loved it just as much as Vicki. This house has been in the Lawson family since the Civil War, and Mona thought of the laughter that used to fill the house when Vicki's grandparents were alive.

The delicious smell of pot pies filled the air as Mona crossed the house to the kitchen. The kitchen hadn't been renovated in over three decades, and Mona was glad that it still felt old fashioned. She grabbed a pot holder and pulled the mini pies out of the oven. They looked as incredible as they smelled. She placed them on a wire rack to cool.

Then, reaching into the cabinet, she selected two mason jar glasses and filled them with ice. She poured lemonade and ice tea and carried the glasses to the front porch where Vicki was already sitting in a high back rocking chair.

"Which one do you want, lemonade or ice tea?" asked Mona.

"I have to go with the lemonade, is that alright with you?" asked Vicki.

"Sure is, you know I love sweet tea."

Mona slumped down on the front porch swing; she wanted to tell Vicki about the police station and the shop, but she wasn't sure where to start, so she blurted out, "What's up with you and Alexander?"

Vicki giggled. "I know you don't care much for him, but we spent the day together yesterday and ended up having burger and shakes at the Burger Barn.

Mona made a face. "Did he pay?"

Vicki smiled. "In fact, he did."

"So, was it a date?"

"Well, we didn't kiss, but the flirting was pretty fun, so I hope so. He's coming over later tonight with some new wine from his shop he wants me to sample." Vicki wiggled her eyebrows at Mona and gave a little woot.

"Uck," Mona said. "Can you find out where he was the morning of the fire, before you get all hot and heavy with him?"

"He didn't set fire to *Jammin' Honey*, Mona!" Vicki said.

"Get his alibi first, then we can decide."

Vicki's smile faded and was replaced by a frown, "I guess you're having a bad day, huh. That stupid article in the paper isn't helping much."

"What article?"

Vicki's eyes widened, and Mona felt sick to her stomach.

"Oh no. What article?" She repeated.

Vicki put the glass of lemonade down on the porch and walked into the house, calling over her shoulder, "Remember, don't kill the messenger." A minute later, she returned with a newspaper. Handing it to Mona, she said, "Take a deep cleansing breath before you read."

Mona held the newspaper in her hand and read the front page. A one-inch tall headline splashed across the page promised exciting inside information into the ongoing *Jammin' Honey* investigation. Mona's eyes jumped from the headline to the paragraphs below, a color picture of her burnt shop covered nearly half the page.

Her hand trembled as she dropped the newspaper on the front

porch, "Vicki, they're accusing me of torching the shop for the insurance money, on the front page. I ought to sue!"

"Mona, I'm so sorry, I thought you knew about it."

"That Mrs. Fletcher called me last night about this rumor, I didn't realize she was serious, that everyone in town thinks I'm an arsonist and a killer. Do they really think that? Vicki, tell me the truth."

"I don't know what to tell you, all I know is that Lacey was at the Burger Barn last night, and she was running her mouth about you to anyone that will listen. She blames you for Collin's death, but Alexander and I are sure it's just her way of coping."

Mona didn't know what bothered her more, that Lacey was out spreading rumors about her or that Vicki was suddenly aligning herself with Alexander as if they were a couple.

"Her way of coping?" Mona asked. "Do you mean to tell me that she'd rather blame me for Collin's death than ask what he was doing in our warehouse? I happen to have heard he was hiding from her!"

"Maybe so, but you can't say anything, she's the widow, it would look bad."

Mona groaned and said, "So everyone in town hates me and thinks I'm to blame for Collin's death because pretty little Lacey says its true, and now the paper prints it, perfect."

"Mona, this will blow over, you just have to give it time."

"I don't want to give it time. I'm innocent, you know that, is there anyone left in town that doesn't consider me a criminal?"

Vicki squeezed. "Of course, there is! I know you didn't set fire to the place. Alexander and Leo know that too. And Aunt Bee—"

"Aunt Bee!" Mona detangled herself from Vicki's grasp. "I forgot! I have to make a few cases of my blackberry ginger jam. Alana from the Coupon Clippers is going to feature it on her blog."

Vicki clapped in childish delight. "That's amazing!"

Mona nodded. "Yeah, it'll help us get some seed money to get a contractor to help rebuild *Jammin' Honey*. We can't just sit around and wait for the insurance people, right?"

Vicki bit her lip and looked uncertain. "Well, I'm glad I made you dinner, now you don't have to cook tonight. Just get busy on those jams."

Mona followed Vicki into her kitchen and happily accepted the pies. She said, "Vicki, I promise you this. I am going to rebuild *Jammin' Honey!*"

CHAPTER 9

*M*ona pulled into her driveway with thoughts bombarding her a mile a minute. On the drive home, she'd realized that she hadn't yet put in an insurance claim and groaned out loud at the thought of all the paperwork.

As she walked up the stairs to her house, she ran a mental to do list, and on top of the list was proving that she was innocent.

Locking the door, she dropped her purse on the kitchen table along with the two mini pot pies and preheated the oven to warm them. She then walked down the hall to the bedroom. Looking in the mirror, she barely recognized herself. The girl she saw that morning who was singing, happy and had perfectly applied her make-up was gone. In her place stood a haggard woman with smeared mascara and a wrinkled blue shirt.

I'm not going to let them get me down!

She pulled her hair into a ponytail and put on a pair of boots. She hiked the short distance to some wild blackberry bushes on her property and harvested several pounds for the jam. Then she returned to her kitchen and donned an apron.

She rinsed the blackberries in the sink, and thought to herself, *I'm going to get back on my feet if it kills me.*

The oven beeped having reached the pre-heated temperature, and Mona put Vicki's pre-made pot pies into the oven to warm.

At least, I have a purpose now. Selling on Alana's blog could be good for her. Thank goodness for Aunt Bee's Coupon Clipper Club. Mona was starting to feel a small glimmer of hope. Aunt Bee believed in her and so did Aunt Cee who'd lent her the money. If she gave up on her dream now, she'd not only be failing herself but her Great Aunts too.

For the first time in hours, Mona smiled to herself.

Forget Leo and his *"she doesn't mean a thing to me."* Forget Lacey and her awful gossip. Forget the stupid newspaper. Mona was strong, feisty and fearless. She would fight for her name, her reputation and her shop.

She put the blackberries, sugar, water, ginger and her special secret ingredients—cardamom and cloves—into a saucepan.

She was startled out of her daydream by the sound of a car coming up the driveway.

She wasn't expecting company, nor did she recognize the sound of the car engine. It didn't sound like Vicki's old beater pickup.

For a moment, she thought of her vulnerability, her house sitting off the road hidden by the trees wasn't safe. Fear surged through her as she thought of what she could use as a weapon in case this was the killer come to finish the job. Reaching into a drawer, she retrieved a butcher knife as the car came to a stop.

Her heartbeat raced as she gripped the handle of the knife. If this was the killer, maybe she would be vindicated. Mona thought of the newspaper headline proclaiming her innocence, but she would first have to survive the encounter.

The car door slammed, and Mona pulled back the curtains, in the fading daylight, she was surprised to see the familiar face of her cousin, Stewart. Judging from the look on his face as he approached the front steps, he didn't look happy. Mona glanced at the knife in her hand and thought about Stewart. She still considered him to be a possible suspect, but meeting him at the door with a knife would be awkward.

Opening a kitchen drawer, Mona threw the knife in and slammed it closed as she walked to the door.

Inviting Stewart in, Mona could sense that he wasn't in the mood to make small talk. His jaw was firmly set, and his mouth formed a frown.

"You've been avoiding me," he said flatly.

"No, I haven't," Mona lied. "Have a seat," she said, inviting him into the living room. "I'll make us some coffee."

He grunted in response and slumped down in a chair.

He's so unpleasant, Mona thought, scurrying off to the kitchen.

"Something sure smells good," Stewart said.

There's no way I'm serving him my dinner! Mona thought.

Maybe I should grab that knife and put him out of his misery!

A few minutes later, Mona brought two cups of coffee into the living room and sat down on the couch across from her cousin, a man who had hardly spoken to her since Aunt Cee had loaned her the money for her shop, six months ago.

"What can I do for you, Stu?" she asked.

"Mona, thank you for the coffee. You didn't have to go through that trouble. I wasn't planning to stay long."

He could have told me that before I made it. What a complete pain he is!

"It was no trouble," Mona said. "The coffee pot does most of the work."

He didn't smile at her joke, instead he said. "Yeah, well, I didn't come here to talk about coffee."

Mona sipped the hot beverage as she thought about what Stewart said, he was baiting her, waiting for her ask him why he was there, in *her* house.

Placing the coffee cup on the table, she studied her cousin before she spoke. He had barely touched the coffee that sat in front of him. His hands gripped the arms of the chair until his knuckles were white, and his facial expression was grim.

"Alright, Stewart, what did you come to talk about?"

"You know damn well what I came for, don't act so innocent."

"What are you talking about? You aren't making any sense. Have you been drinking or something?"

"No, I haven't had a drop. I heard about you and that insurance money. I've got to hand it to you, pretty slick."

"You sound crazy. You can't tell me you believe what they wrote in the paper."

Stewart glared at her as he answered, "You think I'm a fool?" He leaned forward aggressively. "I may have been when I let you outsmart me out of Cecilia's money, but that won't happen again."

Mona's pulse raced, not out of fear. Any fear she'd felt, that perhaps Stewart was the killer and the arsonist, was replaced by anger.

Standing, she said, "Hold on just a second, I've got something to show you that will put that notion out of your head."

Mona stormed out of the living room and walked down the hall to her bedroom. She opened the closet and pulled a box off the shelf. Opening the lid, she pulled out a dog-eared scrapbook. Her emotions were raw.

How can he make me so mad every time we speak?

She inhaled deeply and counted to ten. With so much going on in her life, she wasn't in the mood for an argument. She pressed her free hand to her forehead, a dull headache starting to form.

I can't let him get to me!

She flipped the scrapbook and smiled at the old picture.

There was some clattering in the kitchen and then the sound of the oven opening and closing.

Goodness! How long have I been looking at the photos?

Hugging the scrapbook, she marched out of her bedroom and nearly collided with Stewart in the hallway.

In his hands he held the microscopic remains of Vicki's homemade pot pies. He stuffed what was left happily into his mouth and gave her a cocky smirk. "Yum."

Fury welled in Mona's chest.

I won't give him the satisfaction of telling him he scarfed down my dinner in a single bite.

Pig!

Mona stormed out to the living room and Stewart followed, licking his fingers.

Mona was about to shove the scrapbook into his sticky hands but thought better of it. Instead, she flipped it open and pointed at the pictures. "There, see all those pictures? Where were you? You weren't in them because you weren't there. Look, there is Aunt Bee and Cee at their fiftieth high school anniversary, at church at Easter, making a cake in the kitchen for my birthday, see them?" Mona asked and didn't wait for the answer as she snapped the book shut.

"Those pictures don't mean a thing to me," Stewart said. "You duped Cecelia into thinking you cared about her so she'd loan you the money for your stupid shop. I'm glad at least Bee was smarter than that."

"It's wasn't like that Stewart. No one duped—"

"But I know the truth," Stewart interrupted. "You don't care for anyone but yourself and money. That's why you burned down your shop for the insurance money and killed Collin."

"Stewart, you can't really believe that? You grew up with me and you think that? Tell me why would I burn down my own shop and kill Collin? That doesn't make a lick of sense."

As angry as Mona was with Stewart, she carefully placed the scrapbook on the table as she waited for her cousin to answer. Her dull headache was quickly becoming a throbbing migraine. She had to get him out of her house and get herself to bed.

"I'm not an idiot," Stewart replied with venom. "I know you insured that shop for more than the loan, a lot more. And Collin must have wanted his share, on account of you and he were seeing each other. But I know better than anyone, you don't like to share."

"That too? You believe those rumors? Stewart, you are an idiot, I've never run around with a married man, and the shop was insured, but there's no guarantee I'll ever see a penny of that money."

"That's not what I heard, I heard you were going to be set for life. Especially with old Collin out of the way." Stewart hovered over her. "All I want is what should have been mine. That money Cecelia loaned

71

you should have come to me. And now you are going to get paid again while I struggle to make ends meet, well I ain't having it, do you hear me?"

Mona's vision blurred for a moment, and she shook her head to clear it. She was starting to feel faint.

Dealing with him makes me sick, literally!

"Bottom line, Stewart what the hell do you want? Are you trying to blackmail me?"

"Pay me, give me my fair share. At the very least, you should have hired me for the shop, given me a job."

Mona stood and gave him an answer, "You come into my house, uninvited, accuse me of conning Aunt Cecelia out of her money that she happily loaned me and claim I was running around with Collin, and you think I'm going to give you a dime? You have got to be out of your mind. Now get out of my house!"

"You don't have to tell me twice, I should have known you were too greedy to care about family. No wonder everyone in town hates you," he said as he walked to the door.

"You can tell everyone I don't care about their rumors and innuendo! And for the record, I never slept with Collin, you weasel," Mona said as she watched him leave.

She turned the latch after he left, fuming that he had the gall to come to her house and accuse her of arson, adultery and murder. Sitting on the couch, she flipped through the pages of the scrapbook. There were pictures of Vicki and her grandparents, pictures of Leo and Vicki taken at Christmas back in high school, a picture of Leo smiling into the camera only two days before he started dating Lacey.

Mona put the scrapbook back on the table and carried the coffee cups into the kitchen. Feeling faint, she dropped the cups into the sink. As they broke into several pieces, she tried to concentrate. Her head hurt so badly it was throbbing and she could barely focus, her thoughts were becoming jumbled.

Stewart must have upset me more than I realized.

Holding onto the sink to help keep her balance, she wondered if she was having an anxiety attack.

She stumbled around the kitchen bumping against the stove and feeling the heat from the oven.

She punched angrily at the oven off button, remembering Stewart eating her pot pies and thought, *maybe I just need to eat?*

But she felt nauseous and couldn't stomach any food.

What's wrong with me?

Holding onto the wall for balance, she stumbled into the hallway and gauged the distance to her bedroom. She felt so light-headed she didn't know if she'd make it to her bed.

Then something caught her eye. The cover to smoke detector/carbon monoxide monitor seemed to be on cockeyed. She realized there were no blinking lights or indicators that the device was functioning. She shook her head, trying to clear her jumbled thoughts.

She yanked off the cover, and saw the batteries were missing. She stared at the carbon monoxide detector, trying to make sense of the missing batteries.

I know there were batteries in here ...

Oh my Lord!

Someone's tampered with the monitor!

Suddenly fearing the worst, she stumbled back into the table in the kitchen and reached for her phone. Her head felt ready to explode and she could barely stand as she desperately tried to remain conscious.

I've got to make it outside.

Using all her strength, she put one foot in front of the other and slowly made her way to the door. Heaving open the door, she nearly fell onto the porch. Holding on to a column, she landed on the steps, her eyes nearly shut. Breathing in the fresh air in big gulps, she coughed as the fresh air filled her lungs.

The evening air was cool and smelled of pine, it was also bringing her back from the brink of collapse. With each passing minute of being outside, her head still throbbed with a dull ache, but she no longer felt faint. She remembered the phone, looking around for it, she found it on the front porch.

She must have dropped it as she stumbled outside, she thought as she powered it on. She wasn't sure what to do or who to call, but she was sure that *someone*, was trying to kill her. Shuddering as she stared at the phone, her cousin was the only possible suspect.

Mona reeled at the possibility that her cousin tried to kill her. He was furious and still resentful about the will, but did he truly just attempt to kill her? It was a horrible theory, but the only solution she could come up with, especially with her mind in a fog.

If it was true and Stewart was the culprit, she knew of only one person she could turn to. Even in her present state, she could feel the pain in her chest that came every time her thoughts turned to that one person. She dialed Leo's number and tried to think of him as a police detective and not the man responsible for breaking her heart.

CHAPTER 10

*L*eo arrived at Mona's house about 20 minutes later. He slammed on the brakes in her driveway, dust wrapping around the unmarked police sedan. He was barely out of the car when he yelled to Mona, "Are you alright? Can you breathe?"

Mona's head throbbed in pain, and she propped her head on her elbow in an effort to stay awake. She could not remember ever feeling this exhausted and her head hurting this badly. She nodded her head and spoke, "I'll be fine, now that you are here."

Leo rushed to her side, "You were slurring your words on the phone, I could barely make out what you were saying, I knew something was wrong, so I got here as soon as I could."

Mona looked at him and smiled, "I just called you, I would say you got here pretty darn quick."

"Mona, it's been almost half an hour. Where's the ambulance? They haven't gotten here yet?" He held up his hand and asked, "How many fingers am I holding up?"

"Four, I'm fine, I feel better now."

"What happened? Tell me, take your time while I follow up on the paramedics." He pressed at his phone, dividing his attention between her and it.

Mona put her hand on his arm as she said, "Don't do that, I'm fine."

"I'll be the judge of that. Tell me what happened."

Mona concentrated on the events of the evening; she told Leo about her cousin's visit, his rummaging in the kitchen and eating her pot pies.

"Vicki made them for me. They were gluten-free. He's such a jerk," Mona said, surprised at how whiny she sounded.

Leo put an arm around her and stroked her hair. "Shhh. It's okay. I'm sure Vicki can make you more. Heck, if she gives me the gluten-free recipe I'll make 'em for you."

A warm woozy feeling overcame Mona, and she wondered if it was the carbon monoxide poisoning or Leo holding her close.

"So, he was in my kitchen, you know. Stewart messed with my oven. I'm sure of it."

"What exactly was he upset with you about?"

"He blames me because my Aunt Cecelia loaned me the money for the shop."

"You Great Aunt Cecelia is his grandmother, right?"

Mona nodded. "I guess he's upset because she loaned it to me and not him. But what was he going to do with it? Blow it on a trip to Vegas?"

"Sounds like he has a bit of a grudge, but do you really think Stewart would burn down your shop and then try to kill you in your own home?"

"I don't know," Mona said, shrugging helplessly "I don't like to think that anyone is capable of that."

"I don't either," Leo said, "But I've seen too much to know that they are. Stay here. I'm going to have a look around."

Mona sat on the porch, waiting for Leo to come back, she thought of the rumors circulating about Collin, that could only be the work of one person, Lacey. But Lacey hadn't been here today, only Stewart.

Suddenly she was startled by the loud chirping of her carbon monoxide detector.

Did I only imagine that the batteries had been removed?

Feeling like she was losing her mind, she leaned back against the column as she tried to collect her thoughts.

Leo walked out of the house, and sat down by her side, "I opened the windows to let the house air out. You were right about the carbon monoxide detector, it takes the same batteries as the remote control. The second I put the batteries in, it started going off."

"Good, I mean, I wasn't imagining it."

"No, I found the source of the leak, your oven. I'm not trying to frighten you, but it appears that it has been tampered with. I took a few pictures before shutting off the gas. It looks like you were right, someone may have tried to kill you."

"The only person who has been to my house today was Stewart."

"Were you with him the whole time? Or would he have been able to disable the carbon monoxide detector and tamper with the stove?"

"Well, I did leave him alone for a few minutes while I went to get my scrapbook from the bedroom."

"Interesting, tell me about your day before we jump to conclusions, I know you came to the station this morning. Did you go anywhere else? Give me the timeline of your day."

"I went to the shop," Mona said.

"The shop?" Leo looked startled. "For what? It's a crime scene. You can't go in there."

"No, I didn't go in. I just sort of wallowed around and felt sorry for myself."

Leo's shoulders dropped, and a look of compassion crossed his face. Suddenly he closed the distance between them and took her hands. "I know losing the shop is really tough. But trust me, okay Mona? I'm going to find out who's behind this."

Her heart fluttered for a moment, looking into his eyes, she felt as if she could dive straight into those dark pools, but then she stiffened.

"Trust you? I thought I didn't mean anything to you?"

"What?" Leo asked, confusion clouding his face. "Why would you say that?"

Mona blushed. "I overheard you talking to your chief."

It was Leo's turn to blush. "Mona, I had to say that. Otherwise, he'd have given the case the Larry simpleton Simmons."

Mona laughed at the angst on Leo's face. "Larry, huh?"

Larry had been the valedictorian in Mona's graduating class. He'd left Magnolia Falls to attend Harvard and was sort of a town celebrity. It was no secret he'd always had a crush on Mona, but she rebuffed him regularly.

"Larry is not going to be your hero on this one," Leo said stubbornly.

Warmth swirled in Mona's chest.

He cares!

"Now what about the rest of your day, what did you do?" Leo asked.

"I went to see Vicki and then picked blackberries for my jam," Mona said.

"Sounds productive. I agree that Stewart is the likely suspect, but if you were out most of the day, there was ample opportunity for anyone to have come into your home and tampered with your stove. It's a good thing you didn't turn on the burner or you could have blown yourself up. Those pot pies may have saved your life."

A chill overcame Mona, goose bumps covering her arms. "Leo! I was moments away from turning on the burner! I was about to make a few cases of jam for the Coupon Clippers!"

In her excitement, she reached out and clutched Leo's shirt. He pulled her into him and mumbled something into her hair.

She tilted her face up to his, their lips inches apart.

She didn't dare ask him to repeat what he'd said, only stared into his dark eyes.

Leo hesitated and pulled back from her. He left a hand on her arm and said, "You're cold." He looked off toward the horizon, now getting dark and said, "Where are the paramedics?"

Mona laughed sarcastically, "Probably they read the paper or maybe they heard at The Burger Barn that I'm a terrible person and they don't want—"

Leo frowned. "What happened at The Burger Barn?"

"Vicki told me Lacey was shooting her mouth off about me."

Leo grunted.

"You don't look all that surprised," Mona said.

"I'm not. She can be petty."

"What do you mean? Everyone in town just loves her."

I thought you loved her, Mona thought, although she tried not to let her body language go into jealous rage overdrive.

"Everyone thinks she is such a sweet girl who wouldn't hurt a fly," Mona said.

Leo chuckled and replied with a wink, "They haven't dated her."

"Huh," Mona said. "I thought it was just me, she has hated me since high school for some reason. I don't know why."

"I can tell you why, because all the guys liked you for you, you're genuine, and she's ..." he shrugged. "I don't know, a drama queen. She pretends she's all friendly and chipper, but boy, when she gets you alone, she can make you feel two feet tall. Trust me, that kind of attitude gets old. It took me two years in the desert to get over some of the nonsense she filled my head with."

"Leo, I had no idea."

"No one did. By the way, that information is classified on a strict need to know basis. Don't make me have to kill you, so don't breathe a word of it to anyone. Not even Vicki, got it?"

"Yes sir, I'll take it to my grave."

"Good, if you can stand up I'm going to take you to the emergency room myself. You need treatment for carbon monoxide poisoning, and I need to file a report."

"I don't want to be any bother."

"You aren't a bother, it's important to get this on record, and I want to make sure you are going to be okay."

"If you insist."

"I do, that is a direct order, now come with me."

Mona was still weak as she walked to the car with Leo's help. She watched from the passenger side as he walked around the front of the car, his perfect body illuminated in the headlights, and she couldn't help but start to feel her luck turning around.

I think he might like me!

CHAPTER 11

The next few days were a whirlwind. Leo had offered to post an officer at her house, which Mona had vehemently refused, "Unless, it's you," she'd joked.

While that had made him smile, he'd assured her that as much as he'd have liked to be her bodyguard, he was trying to solidify his standing at the police department and ensure the case wasn't handed off to Larry simpleton, as Leo like to call him.

Fortunately, the days had been non-eventful. Leo had arranged for her oven to be repaired, after he dusted for fingerprints, and Mona had spent the days making Jam for the Coupon Clippers, filing insurance paperwork, and binge-watching *Competition for the Crown*.

On Memorial Day, Vicki had hosted a bar-b-que, but Mona knew Alexander was going to be there and Leo was not, so she'd politely declined.

Today, the sun was shining through the pine trees as Mona walked down the dirt driveway to the mailbox. Opening the box, she was astonished by the piles of junk mail, advertisements and bills that had accumulated over the holiday weekend. Sorting through the envelopes, a letter caught her attention.

Stopping in the middle of the driveway, she juggled the armload of mail and tore open the envelope addressed to her from the insurance company. Butterflies fluttered in her stomach as she scanned the letter.

Oh my goodness. Please be good news! Oh, please be good news!

The investigation was still ongoing, and she was anxious that the insurance company would refuse to cover the damage to the shop.

Reading the letter, she saw that barring any new information or rulings, the insurance company would cover the damage of the fire. The check would be made out to her for the entire amount of the claim to be delivered to her in five to ten business days.

Mona shrieked with joy, dropping several pieces of junk mail. This was the first piece of good news she'd had since before the fire. Bending down, she picked up the mail from the ground and ran to the house. She couldn't wait to share the news with Vicki.

Mona rolled down the windows in her car and played her favorite radio station, singing along with all her favorite songs as she drove to Vicki's house. Pulling into the driveway, she thought she recognized the sedan belonging to Alexander Kaas sitting at the farmhouse.

Ugh! Why is he here? Shouldn't he be opening his shop right about now?"

Mona opened her car door just as Alexander Kaas popped open the front door of Vicki's house. Behind him, Vicki stood in a robe and rumpled hair, holding a steaming mug.

Alexander nodded to her as he walked to his car. Vicki waved from the porch, and Mona watched as Alexander sped down the driveway and out to the road, leaving a swirl of dust in his wake.

"Vicki! It's not getting serious with him, is it?"

Vicki gave her a coquettish smile, as she led Mona into the kitchen. "Maybe. Coffee?"

Mona sat down at the kitchen counter and nodded. Vicki poured her a mug and got busy rummaging around the kitchen. "How are you feeling? Any side-effects from that ghastly carbon monoxide?"

"I'm fine. Much better really. And I've got news. Wonderful news!"

"You do? We could use some good news, come on, out with it while I whip up a batch of lip balm." Vicki pulled out a double boiler from a cabinet and began to fill it with some of her home-harvest honey.

Mona frowned. "Did Aunt Bee hit you up for the Coupon Clippers too?"

"What?" Vicki asked.

"Alana's blog, *Frugalicious*. Is she going to feature your lip balm?"

Vicki laughed as she stirred the boiler, now brimming with sweet smelling honey. "No."

"What are you making the lip balm for then?" Mona asked.

Vicki waved her question off. "First you. Tell me your news and then I'll tell you mine."

Mona nodded. "I got a letter from the insurance company."

Vicki's eyes widened. "And?"

Mona dug the letter out of her purse and fanned it in front of Vicki.

Vicki snatched it out of her hands and tore it open. She scanned the letter quickly and hooted.

"The insurance company is going to send a check to cover the full value of the shop and its contents," Mona shrieked. "Do you know what that means?"

Vicki excitedly grabbed Mona's hands and shrieked back at her. "What does it mean?"

Mona jumped off the kitchen stool. "We're back in business!"

Vicki jumped alongside Mona, the two dancing around the kitchen chanting. "We're back in business! We're back in business!"

Mona paused from the celebration and said, "I'm not saying it's not going to be a ton of work, though, because it is. I've been to the building since the fire, it's a disaster, but not a total loss. We can rebuild. And, if we get the check soon, we can still open this summer. We just have to find the right contractor."

Vicki stared at Mona and for a moment, the bubbling of the sweet-smelling honey in the double boiler was the only sound in the kitchen. Vicki rushed to turn off the stove and removed the honey from the burner. She turned to face Mona and said, "This summer? Isn't that too soon?"

Mona knew her friend and knew how to read her emotions like a book, she replied, "Vicki, what's wrong?"

Vicki glanced from Mona to the double-boiler than back again. "Mona there's something I need to tell you. I didn't think about the shop opening back up, not so soon anyway. With the investigation still open and—"

"Hey wait a minute," Mona said. "You're making a batch of lip balm, and it's not for the Coupon Clippers ... Have you found a way to sell it, did you open an online shop?"

"No, not an online shop," Vicki said. She hesitated, chewing on her lip.

Mona took a step back from. "Don't tell me..." Mona's stomach tightened into a knot as the thought hit her. "It's Alexander, right? What, are you going to go back to selling at his shop?"

Vicki looked down at the floor and said, "Well, I need money, Mona. I can't not sell my products. My financial reserves are drying up, and if I can't make some cash soon, I might have to look at going back to my old job."

Vicki's face was suddenly strained with stress. She'd been a lawyer for a few years after graduating college and Mona knew that Vicki had hated every moment of it. She still remembered the night they decided Vicki would quit her day job and make honey products, and she'd make jam.

It'd been that evening the dream of *Jammin' Honey* had been born, but without the financial wherewithal to open a shop, they'd decided to gain some entrepreneurial experience selling their product at Alexander's Wine and Cheese shop, *As You Slice It*.

Mona tried to make sense of what was happening, to put together the pieces. "But, Vicki, don't you remember how little he paid us. He was giving us pennies on the dollar of every product he moved."

"I know," Vicki said quickly, a rosy blush coloring her cheeks. "But he promised it wouldn't be like that this time."

Anger boiled up in Mona's chest, "Vicki. How could you believe him? Don't you see he's trying to manipulate you!"

"That's not true!" Vicki said, her cheeks going from rosy to red in anger. "We're dating now, and he wouldn't treat me like that."

MONA TOOK A BREATH. "LOOK, I KNOW HE HAS YOU UNDER HIS Svengali spell right now, but don't you find it suspicious that he suddenly developed an overwhelming interest in you after the fire—when your honey products were available once more?"

Vicki loudly disagreed, "That's not true. We've always flirted. He asked me out way back when, but I didn't want to date him while working for him."

Mona huffed impatiently. "And now look! You're dating and working for him!"

The expression on Vicki's face turned from angry to tortured, and Mona suddenly regretted pushing her friend so hard.

She hugged Vicki. "I'm sorry. I don't want to see you get hurt is all. I hope everything works out with you and Alexander, honestly."

CHAPTER 12

*M*ona left Vicki's house, feeling crushed. She had an
awful premonition that things between Vicki and
Alexander wouldn't end well.

The man is a snake.

Mona knew from helping him with the bookkeeping at *As You Slice
It*, that the only reason his shop was ever profitable was because of
Vicki's honey and her own jam.

But Mona feared that if she pressed the issue, she would only
succeed in alienating her friend. For now, it seemed better to let
things sit.

She drove home, with the radio off and window rolled up, the joy
and happiness she felt earlier in the afternoon gone. Clouds bloomed
on the horizon, and the wind buffeted her car about.

A summer squall is on the way. I better get home fast.

Once at home, Mona sorted through the mail that she'd abandoned on the kitchen table when she left to see Vicki. Ripping
through the bills, she gave each of them a cursory glance as she
thought about Vicki. This experience with the fire and Collin's death
had proved to be full of revelations.

She learned that Lacey and Collin's picture-perfect marriage was on the rocks, and that Collin suffered from PTSD in silence. She discovered that Leo and Lacey's relationship wasn't as ideal as she had imagined, that the town thought she was a homewrecker and that Vicki was now hopelessly in love with a hustler.

The fact that her cousin Stewart still resented her for Aunt Cecelia's loan wasn't exactly a revelation, but the fact that he may have tried to kill her was definitely news.

A flash of lightening and the distant sound of thunder warned her that the summer thunderstorm was imminent. As the wind howled through the pine trees, Mona thought again of her vulnerability at home alone.

She shrugged it off with a shiver and tore through the pile of mail. She saw a check she recognized fall out of a plain white envelope. The check was the very one she wrote to Lacey for the catering job. Mona hadn't canceled the job and with the insurance check on the way, she still needed a caterer in the future.

Examining the envelope, she saw no note or letter.

Lacey. What a drama queen.

Although Mona didn't care for Lacey, she wasn't expecting Lacey to have time to pull any shenanigans while she was supposed to be in mourning for her dead husband. As a professional courtesy, Lacey should have sent a note of apology or explanation.

Why am I letting this woman get to me? I don't even like her.

Mona realized that she didn't want to do business with Lacey, but she concluded that canceling the job should have been her decision.

After all, I'm the customer!

Realizing that it was less about Lacey and more about principle, she reached for her phone and called Lacey.

I'm going to let her have it!

But when she got Lacey's voicemail, she decided it was probably better to visit Lacey at the bakery instead of leave an anger-fueled voicemail.

With a loud crash of thunder and a bright flash of lightening, Mona's lights went out. Sitting in the dark with only her cell phone illuminating her small kitchen, Mona said to herself, "Is that mother nature's way of telling me to go to bed?"

Yawning, she checked the locks on the windows and doors, and walked down the hallway to her bedroom.

<><><>

THE NEXT MORNING, MONA WAS AT THE BAKERY BRIGHT AND EARLY. She walked in and asked to see Lacey, half expecting to be told by the teenage girl, Savanna, behind the counter that she wasn't there and wouldn't be back for several weeks.

It's only a few days since Collin's death, maybe Lacey is taking some time off.

Instead, Mona was surprised to find that Lacey was at the Bakery.

Mona waited patiently for Lacey, as she thought about what she would say to her.

There's really no point in starting a fight. I'll still need a caterer when I rebuild Jammin' Honey, and Lacey is the only gluten-free shop in town.

A little voice in Mona's head reminded her that Lacey was the woman responsible for spreading lies and gossip about her around town.

Mona tried to tell the little voice to pipe down!

Even still, she felt anger building as she watched a familiar pretty woman, impeccably dressed walk out of the kitchen.

Lacey looked at Mona, and the tension between the two women was palpable. Lacey broke from her usual pleasant façade and said, "I don't have time for this," as she turned to walk back into the kitchen.

Mona caught up with her as she moved behind the counter, much to the surprise of Savanna, who, like the line of customers, watched the drama unfold in front of their eyes.

"You don't have time for this, or for me?"

"What do you want? I'm busy."

87

"You sent back my check, why? I'm the customer, and I still need a caterer when my shop opens up."

"Are you crazy, I wouldn't cater an event for you if you were the last paying customer in Magnolia Falls."

"Thanks Lacey, way to be professional," Mona said, doing her best to tone down the irate pitch of her voice.

"You're one to talk, you think I don't know what you have been saying about me, prying into my personal life and my marriage to Collin. You were implying that I was responsible for his death, admit it!" Lacey screamed as the bakery became eerily quiet.

"Don't play victim with me, Lacey. You have hated me our whole lives, and you have done everything in your power to ruin my name, spreading rumors about me that I had an affair with your husband. You would love that, wouldn't you? You would love to ruin my name and make yourself look like a victim, that is all you are good at, playing sweet, innocent and now, a victim."

"How do I know you and he weren't seeing each other, he was found dead at your shop, in your warehouse."

"How convenient that you called me, insisting that I leave my shop to come here so you could kill the man, was that the plan, to kill him and let me take the blame?" Mona screamed as years of frustration poured out of her.

"You're crazy! Collin was my husband, why would I kill him?" Lacey asked as she stepped toward Mona.

"I don't know, maybe because Leo came back to town, you never got over him, did you? He left you and you couldn't handle that, not used to rejection are you little miss cheerleader?"

"How dare you say he left me. You don't know what you are talking about. If you don't leave right now, I'll call the cops."

"Go ahead, I don't care. I ought to sue you for slander and defamation of character, so please pick up the phone and call them."

"I'm warning you, you always thought you were smarter than everyone, better than all of us. I guess you aren't so high and mighty now, are you? I heard your best friend has abandoned you." Lacey let out a shrill manic laugh. "She's going back to *As You Slice It*, and just so it can really burn in your craw, I'm supplying bread for the tasting station. Real bread, not that gluten-free cardboard you and Stephanie are so fond of."

Before Mona could respond, Lacey turned and asked Savanna, "Is there anything I've forgotten?"

Savanna gave Lacey a crooked grin, "And Lacey, oh, yes. The tasting station at *As You Slice It* will feature jam."

Mona's hands began to shake in anger and she stuttered. "Wh...what?"

Lacey smiled wickedly. "Uh, how shall I say it? A very special blackberry ginger jam, with just the right about of cardamom and cloves."

Mona's stomach burned as if she'd just been punched in the gut. "My recipes," she whispered. "You stole my recipes!"

Lacey laughed. "Prove it."

For the first time in Mona's life, she actually wanted to strangle another human being. Fury blazed in her heart, and her hands twitched to wrap around Lacey's scrawny neck.

"You're...you're a..." Mona was suddenly aware of the small crowd of people that had front row seats to the confrontation that had been brewing for years. In her mind, she could imagine the front-page headline of the next day's paper reading *Pretty Local Widow Verbally Assaulted by Bitter Adulteress and Local Arsonist.*

Mona held her tongue and rushed out of the bakery. She dashed to her car and sped away.

Where do I go? I have nowhere to go!

As if on autopilot, she drove directly toward the ruins of her shop. Parking the car in the alley way, she took a few minutes to catch her breath. Stepping out into the sunlight, she ducked under the police tape and walked through the remains of *Jammin' Honey.* Taking a critical look at the wreckage, she wondered how long it would take to rebuild it and if it was even worth it.

How did Lacey get my recipes?

Mona choked back tears as she walked through the sad remnants of her kitchen and into the shop where the fire damage was minimal.

Looking at the beams and walls that were still intact, she wondered if it would be worth it to try to rebuild it.

Would I be better off to take the money and leave town, start over somewhere new?

Knowing that her reputation was forever sullied by baseless accusations of felonies and adultery, Mona was frustrated and conflicted about what to do, walking to the pavement in front of the wreckage of her shop, she was consumed with indecision until a bright yellow flyer caught her eye.

Taped to the window of the nearby candy shop, Mona was drawn to the flyer that reminded her of flyers that she had once designed for Alexander's *As You Slice It*. As she drew closer to the flyer, she was certain that it was her old flyer design slightly updated. The flyer announced a gala grand reception at his shop, showcasing some new wines, an assortment of cheeses and announcing a partnership to bring an exclusive line of artisanal honey products and handcrafted jams to the people of Magnolia Falls.

Mona fumed as she tore down the flyer.

Walking back to her car, she stopped once more to gaze at what was left of Jammin' Honey.

Maybe it would be easier to walk away?

CHAPTER 13

*A*ny thoughts of leaving Magnolia Falls evaporated when her phone rang, and the caller I.D. showed Leo.

"Hi," she said, breathlessly, hoping she didn't sound too eager.

"Hey, sorry to bother you," he said.

"Believe me when I say, a call from you is never a bother!" Mona giggled.

Leo chuckled, and the sound sent a shockwave through Mona's body.

God, I love this man!

"I'm calling because I wanted to let you know I brought Stewart in for questioning."

"Oh? You did? And?"

"I don't want to offend you or anything. I know he's family, but—"

Mona laughed. "Go ahead. You won't offend me."

"I don't think he has enough brain cells to orchestrate a fire at your shop and then tamper with your stove. Besides that, he has a pretty air-tight alibi for the fire."

"What's that?" Mona asked.

"He was out gambling that morning. Pulled an all-nighter with some local deadbeat who vouched for him."

"You take the word of a deadbeat?"

"No. But they videotaped their bender and posted it on Youtube. They've all been arrested for the gambling and illegal dope consumption."

"Geez," Mona said.

"Yeah. So, his buddies are pretty irate. I'd say Stu has a target on his back now. But, you know, like I said, he's not the sharpest tool in the shed."

"Thank you for checking it out, Officer."

"My pleasure, my lady."

Ask me out, ask me out, ask me out!

"How are you holding up?"

Mona bit her lip, she certainly didn't want to tell Leo about the face-off with Lacey, instead she said, "I'm okay. Just trying to figure out if I still have a business if Vicki goes back to selling her honey at *As You Slice It.*"

Leo groaned. "I told her not to do that! But you know Mona, it's nothing personal. She needs the money."

Mona pressed her lips together to keep from arguing with him.

What good would that do?

"Hey," he said. "What about the reception thing? I think they're having a tasting on Friday."

Oh my Lord. No, no, no! Don't ask me to go with you.

"Want to be my date?"

Why! Why, why, why?

After all the years of hoping and praying he'd finally asked her out, but it was to go a reception that she'd rather die than attend.

"Mona? Are you there?"

"I ... uh ... I ..." Mona stuttered and wanted to kick herself.

"I'm sorry," Leo said, his voice sounding strained. "I thought ... you know. I thought ... Well, never mind. We can go as friends."

"No, no. Please. It's not that. I'd love to—"

A shrill beep interrupted their call and Mona stared at the phone.

"Sorry, Mona. Dispatch is trying to get through to me. I'll talk to you later."

He hung up so abruptly Mona was left momentarily stunned.
I'm an idiot, she moaned.

<><><>

FOR SEVERAL DAYS AFTER THE SHOWDOWN AT THE BAKERY, MONA
dreaded answering her phone. The town rumor mill was in full force,
and Mrs. Fletcher wouldn't stop calling. Mona didn't want to speak
with her, not after Lacey accused of her of prying into her marriage. It
wasn't difficult for Mona to conclude who had told Lacey about her
inquiries.

When Mona did pick up the phone, she was subjected to being
berated by her family members for Leo questioning Stewart. To
Mona's dismay, she soon discovered that all her cousins rallied
around Stewart believing her to be an arsonist. An aunt on her mother's side had even gone so far as to accuse her of cheating Stewart out
of the loan and now trying to pin the arson of the shop on him.

Mona's nerves were raw, and she felt completely alone. Her best
friend was basically MIA love-shaking with Alexander the traitor, her
cousins had abandoned her, and the entire town thought the worst of
her. Leo hadn't called her since she'd turned down his offer to go the
reception with him and then the fact, that Lacey somehow had gotten
hold of Mona's recipe was the crushing blow.

Mona holed up in her house for days, eating junk food, and binge
watching an entire eight mind-numbing seasons of *Zombie in
Hollywood*.

Finally, the Friday of the reception rolled around, and Mona
stewed about attending. She decided and un-decided so many times
that she made herself dizzy.

The phone rang, but Mona didn't recognize the caller I.D. She
picked it up cautiously and was pleasantly surprised to hear Stephanie
Tyndall on the other end.

"Hey there. I was just calling to check up on you," Stephanie said. "I read in the paper about your argument with Lacey, and I wanted to let you know you're not alone."

Mona grimaced. "There was another article about me?"

Lacey laughed. "Oh, sorry! I thought you knew."

"What did it say this time?"

"The usual garbage. It said you made a grieving widow cry at her bakery."

"Ugh. She didn't cry! And to the tell truth, she doesn't seem all that grieving to me!"

"I know," Lacey agreed. "I think she's more relieved that Colin's gone, than anything."

Mona fumed all over again to think of that day at the bakery. "I might have gotten a little shrill with her, but she deserves it. She stole my jam recipes!"

"She what?"

Before Mona could repeat herself, Stephanie added. "She stole my gluten-free recipes too! That's why I quit."

"You quit?"

"Oh, I know. She likes to tell everyone she fired me. But the truth is, she was selling catering gigs, using my recipes and not giving me any credit. I finally consulted an attorney. And while I couldn't copyright my recipes, he was able to find a loophole that prevented her from using them for anything other than personal use."

"Ah!" Mona cried. "That's why she had to change the recipe!"

"What?"

"She was going to cater my opening, but then told me she had to change the recipes to some garbanzo bean or fava…or I don't know what lie she told me."

Stephanie laughed. "Yeah. Lacey is sort of a pathological liar. She's a piece of work. How did she get hold of your jam recipes?"

Mona sighed. "I have no idea. I thought they were in the shop when it burned down."

After they hung up, Mona stepped out for fresh air and to retrieve the mail.

And then it happened.

In the mailbox was the check from the insurance company. Holding it in her hands, she was torn about what to do. Her first thought was to pack a suitcase, go to the bank, cash the check and head for the airport. Mona fantasized about a tropical island with white sand beaches surrounded by aquamarine water that she would call home.

As she resigned herself to a life of lush palm trees and drinks with umbrellas, she thought about her Aunt Cecilia on her cruise. How could she explain to her the events of the past few weeks? Both Aunt Bee and Cee know Mona wasn't a quitter. And Aunt Cee had not loaned Mona the money so she could squander it living in a tropical island for years. If that was her intention, she could have just given it to Stewart.

I can't let Aunt Cee or myself down. Not while I still have fight left in me.

Thinking of her Great Aunt's strength and unwavering belief that Mona could achieve her dreams, she decided that she would be like Cecilia, who'd thrown caution to the wind and escaped on a whirl-wind cruise around the world.

Cecilia doesn't care what anyone in town thinks of her.

She follows her heart!

With that check, she had enough money to sell her jams and jellies to tourists and not have to worry about breaking even for several years. That gave her plenty of time to figure out what to do about Lacey stealing her proprietary recipes.

Mona wasn't about to let anyone stop her. Especially not whoever was responsible for burning down her shop and trying to ruin her life.

She would make one more valiant effort to rebuild her dream.

He or she is going to have to try harder than that!

Feeling a new sense of purpose sweep over her, she turned off the TV. Opening the pantry door, she reached for a garbage bag and cleaned up the empty snack bags, ice cream containers and candy wrappers from the living room. Soda and beer bottles were next to go as she felt better with each passing minute.

With the check safely tucked into her wallet, she powered on the laptop and started searching for contractors. For a build of this magnitude, she knew she needed a specialist. She combed through the local listings in search of a contractor that could rebuild her kitchen and her business. Scanning the listings, she recognized a familiar name.

Alexander Kaas's name and contact information was displayed on her screen under the heading kitchens, commercial and residential.

Mona read the listing, and suddenly a chill zipped up her spine.

Oh my goodness!

His wine and cheese shop was only one of his business ventures, he hadn't always been a store owner, he had at one time worked with his hands as a contractor. Mona read the information and had a moment of clarity. Without the honey and jam supplied by herself and Vicki, Alexander had to return to doing odd contracting jobs to make ends meet, to afford his lavish lifestyle.

Mona thought about Alexander's specialty, and the police report that the fire at her shop had started in the kitchen and then she was nearly killed in her own home by a leak from her stove that was tampered with by someone.

Was it possible it was Alexander?

Mona remembered the morning of the fire that Alexander had been nearby. He had been outside the blaze, giving her a stupid wave!

How Mona disliked him! He was arrogant, overbearing and had never shown Vicki any attention until now. She knew that he wasn't happy about losing her and Vicki's products to sell at his shop, but she wondered if it was possible that he could have been unhappy enough to commit murder or attempted murder.

Could Alexander be capable of arson just to save his business?

The people who had the most to gain from the fire were Alexander and Lacey.

Lacey had stolen Mona's recipes ... her recipes that had been at *Jammin' Honey* just before the fire ...

In a rush, Mona turned off the computer and looked at her cell phone sitting by the computer. She thought about calling Leo, but she didn't have any concrete evidence against Alexander, just an advertisement and a hunch. Mona knew that wasn't enough to go on, she needed something a little more concrete.

Looking at the clock on the wall, she thought about the reception gala at *As You Slice It* that was scheduled for that evening. Even if Alexander never saw a day behind bars, she was going to make sure that he knew that she was aware of his guilt.

She didn't care what happened after that, her reputation was destroyed and nothing she could do could make it any worse. She had decided that she was going to reopen her shop no matter what anyone in Magnolia Falls thought about it.

If I hurry, I've just enough time to get dressed!

Mona rushed through the shower and selected her best dress, a slinky black wraparound number that she ordered on a whim, online. She piled her hair into a messy up do and lined her eyes in black liner with grey eye shadow for a smoky effect. Berry lip stick, dangly silver earrings and a spritz of perfume completed the look.

Just as she was slipping on a pair of strappy heels, her cell phone buzzed. It was her Aunt Bee calling.

"Darling! The BOGO sale is a great success. Alana says you almost brought the *Frugalicious* server down!"

"I did!"

"Blackberry ginger jam is a knock out!"

"Well, it may have been knocked off too."

"Whatdya mean?" Aunt Bee asked.

"Lacey MacInroy got hold of my recipes, and I understand she's preparing my jam for the *As You Slice It* gala reception tonight."

"Why that little rat!" Aunt Bee said.

"Are you going to the reception?" Mona asked.

"No way! Alexander has never honored, not one of the Coupon Clipper's requests for a sale. Are you going?" Aunt Bee asked.

"Yup. On my way now. Wish me luck," and as Mona hung up, she heard Aunt Bee squeak out, "Luck with what?"

Mona admired her reflection in the mirror and declared herself ready for action. Grabbing her car keys and purse, she nearly stumbled, racing down the front steps. Driving into town, she felt a feeling she had not experienced in a long time, bravery. This new-found liberation from caring about what anyone thought about her was freeing. She felt like her old self once more, that girl she used to be the brave, independent girl that didn't care about reputations and rumors.

The street in front of *As You Slice It* was packed with cars and people dressed for a party.

Wow! He sure does know how to throw a party, I'll give him that.

Mona parked several blocks away and tried to confidently walk in the strappy heels. She soon discovered that a slow gait and not a rushed, hurried pace was best with the pretty but deadly shoes.

Walking down the street, she passed many citizens of Magnolia Falls. She was thrilled that few of them recognized her dressed as she was. Mona was known to be a t-shirt and jeans kind of girl, not a woman who wore high heels and body-conscious slinky dresses. The element of surprise would be useful, she decided, as she walked into the wine and cheese shop.

Remembering to hold her head high, she strolled through the crowd at the shop. In the light of the gala, she was recognized far easier than on the dimly lit street. Her element of surprise wasn't working. Mona no longer cared or needed it, she was in the door, and by the looks of the large crowd, so was nearly everyone else in Magnolia Falls.

As she walked through the crowd, looking for Alexander, she could hear whispers and conversations suddenly coming to a stop. Mona was the center of attention at the gala, she was a local celebrity, now considered infamous and notorious. She decided that she had nothing to lose by making a scene, if necessary.

Uniform waiters worked the crowd, offering slices of Gouda paired with honey and Prosecco, tastes of Dubliner cheese with Cabernet Sauvignon and worst of all a beautiful dry Manchego topped with Blackberry Ginger Jam.

Mona snatched up the Manchego offering and popped it her mouth. While the flavors complemented each other in a heady sort of way, she was relieved to note, that her version of the jam was superior.

Ha! You may have my recipes, Lacey, but you'll never prepare them with my kind of heart!

Despite the crowd, Mona spotted Lacey chatting with a high-profile local politician. She was dressed in a short flashy red dress and squeezing the man's arm as she chugged some wine.

So much for the grieving widow! More like black widow.

Alexander Kaas spotted Mona and stiffened. He was well groomed, impeccably dressed in a pair of pressed khakis, loafers without socks and a coral polo shirt. His long blond hair was slicked back and the gold watch on his wrist caught the light as he moved his arm. At his side was Vicki, dear Vicki who looked like a million bucks.

She was wearing a form-fitting green suede dress with golden trim that created a glow about her as if she'd dipped herself in honey.

She was too good for him!

As Mona drew closer to Alexander, Vicki started to speak but was interrupted by her new boyfriend and business partner.

"Look who we have here?" Alexander said. "If you've come to ask for your old job back, I'm sorry. I'll have to say no. Your jams have been replaced."

A look of confusion cloudy Vicki's pretty face. "What's that suppose to mean?"

Mona wasn't about to be distracted. She motioned to Vicki that they'd catch up later, then smiled sweetly at Alexander. "You and I need to have a conversation. Do you want to do this here or in private, either way suits me just fine."

In the background, Mona heard the melodic strains of jazz music and the silence of a well-dressed crowd that was listening to every word she and Alexander had to say to each other. It seemed that lately, Mona was the center of attention wherever she ventured. Being notorious could be fun if she played her cards right.

Mona glared at Alexander, and her gaze never wavered not even when Leo stepped out of the crowd and placed his hand on her shoulder. Leaning close he whispered to her, "Mona, you look beautiful but what are you up to?"

"Stick around, you'll see," she said to Leo.

"I don't know what business you have with me, if you are mad about Vicki, I suggest you take it up with her another time and not at our reception. Really Mona, this is embarrassing. I'm embarrassed for you that you have sunk this low. I guess what the rumors say about you is true," Alexander said with a smirk.

"Well if that is how you prefer to have our conversation, in full view of the entire town, that suits me just fine. I didn't come here to cause trouble, I came here tonight to tell you something, something that all your guests in their fancy dress clothes may find interesting or not, I really don't care. I just want to tell you that I know it was you, Alexander Kaas, it was you that set fire to my shop and it was you that tried to kill me. You killed Collin MacInroy in the process, but I don't suspect that bothers you."

Alexander turned bright red, as red as the wine he was selling. He looked as though he was going to explode at any second. He turned to Leo and demanded, "You're a cop, I want her gone, I want her out of my shop this instant, do you hear me?"

Mona looked at Leo, waiting for him to grab her by the arm and kick her out into the street. He didn't, he turned to Alexander and said, "I'm a cop, that is true, but I'm interested to hear what she has to say before I remove her from the premises."

Without hesitation, Mona replied, "Alexander, don't play innocent with me, I know you specialize in kitchen installations and ovens, even oven repair. I believe it was no coincidence that the fire at my shop started in the kitchen caused by the stove and then the attempt on my life was due to tampering with my stove and the disabling of my carbon monoxide alarm. You had the expertise and the opportunity to do both."

Alexander chuckled, "Why in the world would I do that? I don't have a motive, without a motive you don't have a case, do you?"

"That's where you're wrong, you do have a motive. Remember I worked for you, I used to keep your books, I know how much money Vicki and I made for you. I know without us you would be broke and must close your business. You needed us, our jam and honey, the product of our hard work and sweat was the only thing that made a profit for you. I know how you see yourself with your nice clothes and snooty attitude. You didn't want to have to go back to being a contractor. You wanted us to fail and come crawling back to you," Mona said.

Vicki reddened, then said, "I suppose one of us did."

"I've heard enough, that is it, I'm asking you to leave my shop and don't come back or I'll have you arrested for trespassing. Do you hear me?"

"But there's one more thing," Mona said. "I have proof that you were there. My recipe book was at Jammin' Honey before the fire. It should have been destroyed. But you took it and gave to Lacey. Am I right?"

Alexander paled and looked around the room for Lacey, who was just slipping out the back door. The guests whispered and started slowly stepping away from Alexander and Vicki. Leo turned to Mona and asked, "Is that true, the books, the profit margin, all of it?"

"It sure is, every word."

"This is ridiculous, you come in here and try to ruin my grand opening. I don't have to stand here and listen to any more of this."

"You are right Mr. Kaas, you don't have to stand here and listen to any more of this, if you will accompany me to the station, I have a few questions I would like to ask you."

Mona smiled, and Vicki came to over to link her arm through Mona's. Together, they walked away. They walked past people that Mona knew from town, people that gossiped about her and spread rumors. As they walked toward the door, a waiter stopped them and offered a tray of sparkling wine flutes. Mona and Vicki both grabbed a glass and toasted to themselves.

CHAPTER 14

$\mathcal{M}$ona drank a cup of coffee as she sat on the front steps of her mountain home, the newspaper folded neatly at her side. The front page of the Magnolia Falls Gazette featured a large headline that read, "Local Cheese Shop Owner charged in Jam Shop Fire." For Mona, it was vindication, the nightmare was over, she was no longer a suspect in the accidental death and the fire that destroyed her business. Butterflies lazily flitted among the honeysuckle in the warm morning breeze as Mona watched, feeling the tension leaving her body.

It is finally over, I can start over.

The experience was enlightening for Mona, she learned the hard way who her real friends were, what her family thought of her and who she could count on as she faced allegations and public ridicule. She knew that she would never see many of her fellow citizens of Magnolia Falls the same way again, but she no longer let that worry her; she had other, better thoughts to occupy her mind.

Losing the *Jammin' Honey* shop was a trial that nearly broke Mona, but she persevered, emerging from the ordeal with a brand-new plan. No longer content to rely on the taciturn loyalty of local customers, she made the decision that she would rebuild and re-open a brick and mortar shop for the tourists. This time, she wasn't content to stop at just owning a shop. Her new business plan included investing in online distribution and selling her jams through select retailers in larger cities.

She also realized that jam and honey were perfect compliments to bread and crackers. And when baked by the right person, gluten-free didn't have to taste like cardboard. So, the new and improved *Jammin' Honey* would now include a bakery and be called *Jammin' Honey Buns.*

And as for cousin, Stewart, Mona had apologized for suspecting him of terrible things, and in order to make amends, had offered to help him to secure the lease for the shop that had previously been Alexander's store, *As You Slice It.* Cousin Stewart was looking forward to the opportunity to make something of himself. And, Aunt Bee had agreed to supervise his books to be sure he didn't overspend. That had made Mona and Vicki smile, but Stewart groan.

If the fire hadn't happened, she would never have considered other avenues for sales, but the fire did happen, and Mona could look back on the tragedy as giving her the motivation she needed to be bold and fearlessly promote her brand. The public ridicule and slander was difficult to bear, but it was the death of Collin MacInroy that was the true tragedy.

Mona hadn't been close to him, but she mourned him and prayed that his suffering was over, that he had found peace. As a tribute to Collin, she made the decision to donate a portion of the business's profits to charities that helped veterans suffering from PTSD. It was a decision that was cheerfully supported by *Jammin' Honey Bun's* newest employee, Stephanie Tyndall.

Hiring Stephanie Tyndall was one of the best decisions Mona had ever made. Stephanie was passionate about baking and using the highest quality ingredients, no cutting corners like Mona knew Lacey was prone to do.

Lacey had gotten off with minimal punishment. She'd told the judge that she never knew about Alexander's plans to burn down *Jammin' Honey* and was surprised when he'd offered her Mona's trea-sured recipe book.

The judge was sympathetic but firm. He sentenced the grieving woman to a year of community service. She also had to return the recipe book to Mona and promise never to sell a single pot of jam.

With thoughts of the grand opening quickly approaching, Mona rushed around the house, careful not to wrinkle the paper under her arm, it was a keepsake she wanted to frame one day. Nearly tripping over the stacks of boxes containing jars of jelly, she set the coffee cup on the counter and raced down the hall, hoping to get a quick shower before heading off to meet the contractor at *Jammin' Honey Buns*.

Still damp from the shower, Mona dressed quickly in her uniform of choice, jeans, t-shirt and flip flops. A light coat of moisturizer and lip gloss were all the make-up she chose to wear as she surveyed her reflection in the bathroom mirror. Her hair pulled back in a ponytail, she was pleased to see the bags under her eyes were fading; she was returning to her old carefree self.

Mona grabbed her purse and car keys and walked down the front steps to her car humming a song; her heart was lighter than it had been in a long time. As she turned the key in the ignition, she switched on the radio. Singing along with her favorite song, she was optimistic that the contractor would tell her good news as she drove toward town.

Once at the shop, Mona was surprised to see Vicki already there speaking with the contractor, Mark Harding.

Stephanie had recommended him. He was a handsome man, in his late thirties and unmarried. He had a great work ethic, good reviews and a warm personality.

Better yet, Vicki seemed to really like him, and Mona knew he was a lot better catch than Alexander Kaas could ever have been.

With a little luck and a lot of hard work, they'd be ready to reopen the shop, July 4th.

The little bell over the door chimed, and as it opened they all turned to see Leo walk into the shop.

Mona nervously tucked a strand of hair behind her ear, "Detective, have you stopped by to inspect the premises, making sure we don't have another untimely fire?"

"I don't want to see history repeat itself."

"We'll install an emergency sprinkler system," Mark said.

Leo nodded at him. "That's an excellent idea."

As the men chatted, Vicki leaned over and whispered into Mona's ear. "I like Mark, let's hire him."

Mona looked from her friend to the new contractor, then to Leo. She smiled, and said, *"Jammin' Honey Buns* will be open soon, and I predict a very sweet beginning.

The End

* * *

hank you for reading Murder as Sticky as Jam. I hope you enjoyed Mona's story as much as I did writing it. The next book in the Cooking up Murder series continues Mona's friendship with Vicki and gets her one-step closer to a romance with Leo... maybe...lolyou have to read and see! You can get Murder as Sweet as Honey here.

And if you'd like some bonus recipes and a sneak peek at Murder as Sweet as Honey...just turn the page.

BONUS SELECT RECIPES – FROM A GLUTEN-FREE PALATE

I hope you enjoyed *Jammin' Honey*. Below are a few recipes from my dear friend, Chrystal Carver's gluten-free website. For more wonderful recipes you can visit her at A Gluten-Free Palate

GLUTEN-FREE SOUTHERN BISCUITS

INGREDIENTS:

- 1/3 cup gluten-free all purpose flour blend (see below)
- 1 cup cornstarch
- 2 teaspoons gluten-free baking powder
- 1/2 teaspoon baking soda
- 2 teaspoons granulated sugar
- 1/2 teaspoon salt
- 1 teaspoon xanthan gum
- 5 tablespoons butter, cold**
- 3/4 cup buttermilk**

- **Substitution Solution: Substitute the buttermilk with rice milk + 1 teaspoon white vinegar and the butter with a vegan

butter and make these dairy free and vegan! Note:
Substitutions may change the texture and flavors slightly.

Instructions:

1. Preheat oven to 375°F (190°C). Lightly grease a baking pan;
   set aside.
2. In a large mixing bowl sift together the first seven
   ingredients. Cut in butter with fork or pastry cutter until
   mixture resembles coarse crumbs.
3. Add buttermilk (or rice milk + vinegar) to the flour mixture,
   while stirring with a fork. Stir just until dough is moist and
   pulls away from the side of the bowl.
4. Sprinkle flour on a piece of wax paper, spoon the dough on
   top of the flour into one ball, and flour the top of the dough.
   Place a piece of wax paper on top of the dough and roll it
   out. It should be about 1 inch think. Cut dough with a
   floured biscuit or cookie cutter. Press together unused
   dough and repeat rolling and cutting procedure.
5. Place biscuits on the baking sheet and bake for 20-25
   minutes or until golden brown. Makes 8 biscuits.

All-purpose gluten-free flour blend – Yields 4 cups
   2 cups white rice flour
   1 cup tapioca flour
   1 cup potato starch
Directions: Mix all the ingredients in a large zipper storage bag or
a bowl. Store flour blend in an airtight container. Shake the container
before using in case any flours have settled.
   Grain-Free Strawberry Thumbprint Cookies
   Ingredients:

   • 2 cups pecans
   • 3 tablespoons pure maple syrup (or honey)
   • 1/2 teaspoon gluten-free baking powder

- 1/4 teaspoon salt
- no sugar added strawberry preserves

Instructions:

1. Preheat oven to 350°F (180°C). Line a baking sheet with parchment paper; set aside.
2. Place the pecans in a food processor and processes for 1-2 minutes or until the pecans start to turn to butter. You should see the pecans near the bottom of the processor turn to pecan "butter". The pecans at the top of the processor should resemble pecan meal or pecan flour.
3. Add the maple syrup, baking powder, and salt. Process for an additional 20-30 seconds or until your dough forms a ball.
4. Using a cookie scoop (or a tablespoon), scoop out cookie dough balls approximately 1 inch thick.
5. Place them on your parchment lined cookie sheet 2 inches apart. Press the center with your thumb, or the back of a spoon, until you make a small crater.
6. Place 1/2 teaspoon of strawberry preserves in the center of each cookie crater.
7. Bake in the oven for 15 minutes.
8. Cool completely before removing from the cookie sheet.
9. Store in an airtight container at room temperature.

For more wonderful recipes, visit A Gluten-Free Palate

READY FOR MORE?

ook 2 from Cooking up Murder Available Now...

Click here to get your copy now.

MURDER AS SWEET AS HONEY

CHAPTER 1

*V*icki Lawson pulled into the parking lot three minutes late. That was fashionably late, right? She took a breath as she grabbed her wicker basket of samples.

"Breathe," she whispered. "This will go great."

She'd known it was a long shot when she dialed the phone number on the flyer. After last year's debacle, she hadn't expected to get a booth at the Fall Festival—Julia, the festival chair, had absolutely hated Mona's jam and Vicki's honey and had sent them packing. Her exact words had been something like, "You'll get a booth here over my dead body."

But Vicki had decided to try again this year—she and her best friend, Mona, *needed* a venue to sell their products while Jammin' Honey was being rebuilt. If Vicki could move some of her products at the Fall Festival, she'd buy herself—and her dwindling savings account—a little more time.

And the long shot might be about to pay off. When Vicki had called, she'd found out that Julia wasn't the festival chair this year, and that the new chair would be delighted to take a look at Vicki's samples.

Vicki opened the car door and headed toward the warehouse.

The exterior of the warehouse looked festival ready. Straw bales and pumpkins lined the outside, alongside a few scarecrows. Some leaves were scattered by the entrance, and a large sign on the roof announced the dates of the festival.

Pretty good advertising, Vicki thought. *I feel festive already!*

Then Vicki caught sight of Julia near the corner of the building.

Less festive, now. What's she doing here?

Julia was tall, with chestnut hair and an impeccable sense of fashion. Today, her hair was pulled back into a ponytail, and her belted coat and skinny jeans looked effortlessly put together. But Vicki only had time to feel a flash of envy at Julia's sartorial sensibilities.

Something wasn't right.

Julia was gesticulating wildly, arguing with an older man. By the time Vicki drew near the door, the man had stormed off. Julia whirled around and caught sight of Vicki, and her face reddened.

"Hey, Vicki," Julia called, striding toward her.

Vicki paused, unsure what to do. Why was Julia even here if she wasn't the festival chair?

"Um . . ." Julia reached her. "That was my stepdad. He wants to sell his paintings at the festival."

"Oh." Vicki opened the door halfway. "I thought Kristen was coordinating it this year."

Julia glowered. "She is, but I'm the deputy chair. And I won't have his paintings here. They're not very good, and he prices them way too high."

Vicki stayed where she was and let the door swing closed. *Julia seems . . . really upset.* Despite her profound dislike for the woman, a kernel of sympathy bloomed in her chest.

"He kept saying these paintings were different, that he'd price them reasonably and that he wasn't as protective of them, but I know how he is about his stupid art. I can't have him in the festival," Julia said. "We can't be responsible for them. If one of his paintings got damaged or stolen . . . well, he'd have a fit."

"That looked like more than a painting issue," said Vicki slowly. "Is everything okay? It seemed pretty heated."

Julia scoffed, but her chin trembled. "Family. You know the drill."

"Family?" Vicki probed.

"My mom's sick." Julia stopped, looking almost surprised that the words had come out of her mouth. "Never mind me and my problems. It's not a big deal. What are you doing here?"

It seemed like a big deal. But Vicki decided to keep that observation to herself. "I'm here to talk to Kristen. She invited me to bring samples over."

Julia looked at the basket, rolled her eyes, and shoved the door open. Vicki followed her inside.

A spacious room opened up before her, the exposed wiring and piping along the ceiling offering a casually trendy ambiance.

Halfway across the space, a flannel-clad woman with braided red hair was laying down some papers, spacing each sheet about ten feet apart. She glanced toward Vicki and Julia and waved.

"Vicki?" she called.

Vicki nodded, then sneezed. The light streaming in from a set of high windows illuminated the floating dust motes.

The woman jogged in her direction and stuck out her hand. "I'm Kristen. Just mapping out vendor stalls. This is our first year in this space, and they let us come in early."

Vicki shook Kristen's hand. "So good to meet you."

Kristen pointed to a nearby table covered in a decade of dust. "Yikes. This place needs a cleaning. But why don't you put your basket there, if you don't mind, and we'll take a look at your samples." Then she glanced quizzically at Julia. "Who was yelling just now?"

"Frank was harassing me again," moaned Julia.

Kristen rested a hand on Julia's upper back, and they stepped away, Kristen's voice becoming soothing.

While they were talking, Vicki placed her baskets on the table and pulled out a handful of sample tins. After a minute, Julia and Kristen returned to the table.

"Here are the samples," Vicki said to Kristen.

Before Kristen could reach them or say anything, Julia snatched a tin of the relaxing body scrub, opened it, and sniffed. She wrinkled her nose and muttered, "I wouldn't put this crap in the festival."

Molten frustration welled up in Vicki's chest. *Well, I wouldn't put your crappy attitude in the festival.*

"Oh!" Kristen's eyes widened, and she snapped her fingers as if she'd forgotten something. "I'm an idiot. Julia, could you run down the street to the bank and get the last five month's transactions for the festival account? I was supposed to print those off this morning. I need to see if a sponsor's check has cleared. They called me up yesterday and asked if I would look into it. It cleared a while ago, but they're old-school, and I want to be able to show them a physical paper trail when they come by this afternoon."

"Fine," huffed Julia. She grabbed her purse and stalked out the door.

As soon as the door closed behind her, Kristen shot Vicki a conspiratorial grin. "That should give us some time."

Vicki smiled back. She liked Kristen's style.

"So, what do we have in the baskets?" asked Kristen. "Well, I assume jam and honey? Julia mentioned something about the honey situation from last year. She . . . can be a bit much, can't she?"

Vicki breathed a sigh of relief and searched for something diplomatic. "I like Julia, but her tastes and mine don't necessarily jive."

Kristen laughed aloud. "My tastes don't jive with Julia's either. I think she just doesn't like jam, to be honest. In the years she ran the festival, she rarely let any vendors sell jam. I, however, enjoy it just fine—and even if I didn't, I'm aware enough to know that someone else might."

Tin by tin, Vicki handed over the samples. She held her breath as Kristen smelled the two body scrubs and tasted Vicki's cinnamon honey and Mona's jam.

"Where do you get your supply of honey?" Kristen asked.

"I have my own beehives," said Vicki, running her thumb along the rim of the wicker basket. Kristen looked impressed, so she added, "I also grow and dry my own herbs."

"This is what I call *good* quality," said Kristen, tucking the last tin back inside the basket. "I would love to have you sell your goods at the Fall Festival."

Yes! Vicki forced herself to maintain a professional grin rather than break out into a disco celebration. "Thank you," she said. "I hope Julia doesn't give you too much grief about that."

Kristen waved a dismissive hand. "Ignore Julia. She's had a tough few years with her family problems. You saw how crazy her stepdad is."

Vicki hesitated. "I don't mean to pry, but . . ."

"But anyone would be curious after the yelling display they put on out there?" Kristen said with a knowing look.

Vicki nodded sheepishly.

"Well"—Kristen glanced back and forth as if to make sure no one was near enough to overhear them, though they were the only two people in the warehouse—"Julia's mom has been very sick for a few years. Julia's stepdad wants her to drop everything and wait on her mother hand and foot. Like, he wants her to stay at home and take care of her mom because it's a *daughter's duty*, or something. Now, Julia isn't an only child. She has a brother who'd be happy to help. But her stepdad insists that it's Julia's job and *only* Julia's job. He's already gone behind Julia's back once and gotten her demoted to second-in-charge of the festival. Even told her afterward that she should have more time to look after her mom now."

"He sounds like a real winner," said Vicki sarcastically. *Might explain why Julia has been so mean. She has her own problems.*

"Julia even offered to pay for a live-in nurse. And it's not like she doesn't see her mom! She's there literally every day—she just doesn't want to spend every single minute there. But the idea that Julia would leave her mom's bedside for even five minutes sends the man into an uproar."

"Wow, you'd think he'd appreciate Julia's offer to pay for a nurse." Vicki picked up the basket.

"You'd think." Kristen tapped her fingers on the table and glared at the door. "But he's crazy. He's so insistent that Julia be at home with her mom that he's threatened to ruin the Fall Festival."

MURDER AS SWEET AS HONEY

CHAPTER 2

"Mona, we're in the festival!" Vicki exclaimed when her best friend answered the phone.

"What? Are you serious?" Mona shrieked.

"Yes, it opens in a couple weeks. I can have a bunch of stuff ready by then. How about you?" Vicki buckled her seat belt and leaned back against the headrest, giddy.

"I should be able to work on some new jams this weekend," said Mona breathlessly. "How about we do a fall theme?"

"You read my mind." Vicki broke out into a dance in her seat. "I already have some cinnamon and pumpkin-spice honey sticks."

"I could make some muscadine jam and apple butter. And some strawberry and blueberry jam to fill out the table."

Vicki's mouth watered. "That sounds delicious! I'll have my body scrubs, some lip balm, and my honey straws. I might take along some honeycomb too. I'll be harvesting tomorrow after Coupon Clippers."

"Mmm, I love your honeycomb. Did you know that beeswax is being sold at some festivals now?"

"Beeswax, huh? Where'd you see that?"

"At the county fair last weekend. The guy selling it had some candles, but also just the plain beeswax. He said people are using it to coat their tools, and cheesemakers use it to cover their cheese."

"Interesting," she said slowly. "Beeswax is the main ingredient in most of my products, but I could bring along a few pieces of plain beeswax too."

"Cool," said Mona. "Oh, could I buy one of your relaxing scrubs? I could sure use all the help I can get to keep my stress levels down. These contractors working on my store are so flaky it might kill me."

"I'll give you a jar," promised Vicki.

"No, that'll cut into your profits."

"It's okay." Vicki grinned, even though Mona couldn't see her. "I'm doing it for a selfish reason."

"Hmm?"

"Because I'd love some of your muscadine jam!"

"Consider it a trade. I'll bring a jar to Coupon Clippers tomorrow!"

They hung up, and Vicki checked an incoming text message. It was from her brother, Leo. *Hey, we still on for dinner?*

Of course, she replied. *See you in a few hours!*

* * *

THE CHILLY AFTERNOON AIR SIGNALED AUTUMN WAS UPON MAGNOLIA Falls. From her barstool perch in her homey kitchen, Vicki squinted down at the glass bowl on the counter. "Let's see . . . just a little more peppermint oil. That should do the trick," she murmured. She unscrewed the bottle of peppermint oil and filled the dropper.

"One, two, three . . ." she whispered, counting each drop.

This was it. She could feel it. Once she put the finishing touches on her line of honey body scrubs, she could really try to make this business work. The Fall Festival would be the first big test.

She glanced out the window, at the beehives on the far side of the yard. Her first venture into the honey business had gone up in flames —literally—when her best friend's store had burned down shortly before the grand opening. Before the fire, Mona had been planning to feature Vicki's products. Now, neither friend had much of a functioning business. Sure, they had online stores, but Vicki's certainly didn't come close to making ends meet.

Her throat tightened at the thought of checking the balance in her savings account.

But these scrubs—and the Fall Festival—were going to be her big break.

I can practically smell the success! Vicki thought.

Or maybe that's just the peppermint.

The peppermint overpowered the kitchen, even masking the spicy smell of the simmering stew on the back burner.

Ventilation!

She opened the window halfway, letting in the crisp, clean air.

From outside came an emphatic *quack.*

Vicki peered down at the grassy lawn. "What's that, Sunny? Is that enough peppermint?"

She picked up the bottle to recap it, but a thin sheen of oil on the glass made it slippery. The tiny jar slipped through her fingers and fell straight into the body scrub mixture. With a little shriek, she snatched it back up and held it up to the light. It didn't look like too much had spilled. But the scrub *definitely* had enough peppermint now.

Sunny, her pet duck, quacked in reply and shook her white tail feathers.

"Good girl!" Vicki closed the bottle securely, then wiped her hands on a navy kitchen towel and reached for the bowl of blueberries she kept close at hand. She tossed a berry out the window, and Sunny swerved to chase it down.

"You're all sunshine, huh?" Vicki had adopted Sunny after her latest romantic interest had ended up in jail for burning down Mona's store and killing someone in the process. Adopting a duck was more of a commitment than any of the standard breakup scripts, like changing her hair or buying pints of Ben & Jerry's by the armful or learning how to swordfight, but Vicki had loved every minute of being a duck mom.

Sunny waddled over to the kitchen window and gazed up hopefully.

Vicki tossed her another blueberry. Then the oven beeped, announcing it was done preheating. She glanced up at the wall clock. "Your Uncle Leo's going to be here soon!" she said to Sunny. "It's time to put the cornbread in the oven and make the salad."

She opened the preheated oven and set the glass pan of cornbread batter on the rack. Then she grabbed a bagged Caesar salad from the fridge and tossed it.

Turning her attention back to her scrub mixture, she murmured. "Now, where were we?"

She bent over and sniffed the mixture, and the overwhelming scent of peppermint wafted over her. She grabbed a wooden spoon and started stirring. After a couple minutes, she squinted down at the scrub.

"I think that should do it," she said, setting aside the wooden spoon. She glanced out at the yard, but Sunny had wandered back to her makeshift pond in a children's plastic wading pool. With a half sigh, Vicki tapped the edge of the bowl. "Guess I better test this scrub out if I'm going to be giving samples to the coupon queens tomorrow."

She carried the peppermint scrub—she'd call this one her *energizing blend* until she came up with a clever name for it—up the stairs and into the bathroom.

"Self-care, for the win." Vicki set down the bowl and smoothed some of the scrub on her arms. Warmth tingled over her skin.

This feels good.

Her skin got hotter and hotter. Too hot. Vicki let out a yelp and dove for the sink. She turned on the cold water and washed the scrub off her arms.

Still feels a bit tingly. Guess that was too much peppermint oil.

She blew on her arms to cool them down.

The doorbell rang, and her eyes widened. Leo was early!

"Coming!" she yelled, toweling-drying her arms and jogging down the stairs. She threw open the front door to greet her big brother. "Leo!"

From the backyard, Sunny quacked frantically.

Leo chuckled and gave Vicki a quick hug. "Sounds like DuckTales back there wants to say hi."

"She always does."

Was that *gel* in his hair? Leo never paid much attention to how he looked, but today his hair was slicked back and he looked downright dashing in his well-fitted button-up.

Interesting.

Vicki closed the door and led Leo into the kitchen. He looked around and seemed to deflate a little. "Just us?" he said. "Mona's not here?"

Vicki bit back a grin. So *that* was why he'd taken a little more time with his appearance. "She couldn't come today. She got tied up waiting for the construction manager at the store. That rebuild has been a headache and a half."

"Oh, did that Mark guy not work out? The contractor?"

"No. And too bad. He was cute." She looked up at the clock. "Lunch is almost done. Cornbread will be out of the oven in fifteen minutes."

"Everything okay?" Leo asked after a long pause, studying her.

Vicki bustled to the stove and tasted the stew to check how it was coming along. Savory and delicious, just like the recipe had promised. "Aww, were you worried about me?"

Leo could read her better than anyone, and he always did feel like he needed to protect her. Plus, after what had happened with her last boyfriend, that big-brother instinct wasn't going away anytime soon. Not to mention that he was a cop *and* ex-military, she thought wryly. No, there would be no dissuading him from the idea that he needed to keep an eye on her.

Leo just shrugged, then peered through the half-open window at the fluffy, white duck. "Hey, Sunny," he said, tapping the glass pane. Sunny quacked.

"So, can I call you a crazy duck lady?" he asked with an amused grin.

Vicki rolled her eyes. "Very funny. As a matter of fact, I have *news!*" She sang the last word.

"Oh?"

A huge grin overtook her face. "We're in the Fall Festival! Mona and I snagged a booth!"

"Bam!" He gave her a high five. "That's amazing! As soon as you said that awful chair lady wasn't in charge anymore, I knew you'd get in. You'll outsell all the other vendors."

Vicki warmed at the compliment. "Well, it'll definitely be a lot of work to put it all together, but I'm excited about the challenge."

His nose wrinkled. "So, is that why it smells like a candy cane factory exploded in here? New product?"

"Oh! I was just putting the finishing touches on my energizing body scrub. Aunt Bee practically commanded me to bring samples to Coupon Clippers tomorrow. I tried some right before you got here."

He eyed her suspiciously.

"What are you laughing at?" She crossed her arms.

He held up his hands in surrender. "Not laughing! It's just . . . did you try it on your arms?"

"Yeah," she said. "Why?"

Leo pointed to her arms.

She looked down and gasped. They were bright red! *How . . .*

The spilled peppermint oil. She must have spilled a *lot*.

Her hand flew to her mouth, and she burst out laughing. "Guess I put a *little* too much peppermint oil in this batch."

"You think?" Leo asked. "Does it hurt?"

"It burned when I put it on, but I washed it off right away. Feels fine now."

His lips quirked in amused concern. "Seems like you could use some help."

That unexpected anxiety curled in her stomach again. Yes, she needed help. Because if she couldn't get this business off the ground, it was back to the soul-sucking days in the courtroom. But she turned on a cheery smile. "Would you like to sample the next batch?"

Leo scoffed. "No way. I can't go into work looking like I have second-degree burns. They'd stick me at a desk."

"Just tell them it was one of your crazy sister's concoctions," said Vicki with a grin.

"Like the soap that tinged my face green?"

"The guys understood that was my fault, right?" She affected an innocent face.

"Didn't stop them from calling me Grinch for the next two days. No," he said, leaning back against the counter with his arms crossed. "I'm done being your guinea pig. Find someone else to torment."

"You know you'll help me out in a pinch."

"Yeah, right."

"That's what brothers are for!"

Leo laughed and reached out to mess up her hair like she was still twelve. He'd have her back no matter what, and they both knew it.

"All right," he said, "I'll help. Besides being your guinea pig or dumping out all your peppermint oil, what can I do?"

"Well, as you know, I learn from my mistakes, so . . ." She glanced at the clock again. "I think we have just enough time before the cornbread comes out. I'm going to whip up another batch of the energizing scrub. Could you grind up the fresh ginger root and astragalus?" She pointed to some dried herbs on the counter.

"Sure," said Leo, grabbing the herbs. He ground them with a mortar and pestle while Vicki mixed the oils, honey, and salt.

"Hope you didn't accidentally add peppermint to the cornbread," he quipped.

With a snort, Vicki said, "The cornbread came straight out of the box, as God intended. I only added milk, butter, eggs, and a little honey from my hives. But I made the stew from scratch, so that's what you should be worried about."

"I'm terrified to try it," he replied dryly. "So, Aunt Bee roped you into Coupon Clippers?"

Vicki reached into the bowl to test the consistency of the scrub, her nose twitching. "Yeah, maybe a month ago. You try telling Aunt Bee *no* when she puts her mind to something."

He laughed aloud. "I wouldn't dare."

Technically, Bee was Mona's aunt, but pretty much everyone called her Aunt Bee. The formidable woman always meant well, but her chief joys in life were clipping coupons and giving opinions. Lots and lots of opinions.

"She wouldn't take no for an answer, and said"—her voice took on an affectionate mimicry of Aunt Bee's dramatic warble—"*I know you need to start pinching pennies, especially after the fire.*"

"She didn't!" Leo cried, nearly dropping the pestle.

"She did," Vicki groaned, affecting wry horror so that Leo wouldn't see the panic rising in her throat. If this business didn't work out, she'd have to go back to being a lawyer.

That wouldn't be *so* bad, right?

But she couldn't even convince herself.

She took the herbs Leo had ground and started mixing them into the scrub with a vengeance. She'd just gotten so tired of seeing criminals go free. She wanted to live a quiet, happy life with her duck and her bees. That sounded like some real peace. Way better than working in the court system. The thought of going back to lawyering exhausted her all the way to her bones.

No. She wouldn't have to go back to being a lawyer. She'd *pinch pennies*, in Aunt Bee's words, until she made this business work.

She had to.

MURDER AS SWEET AS HONEY

CHAPTER 3

By the time Vicki and Leo finished the scrub, anticipation pulsed through her.

"Time to test it!" she cried, snatching the bowl from the counter.

"Hold on," said Leo, his face a picture of resignation. "You've already given yourself a sunburn. Let me try it on one of my arms."

"Are you sure, Grinch? You swore you were done being my guinea pig," Vicki teased.

Leo rolled his eyes. "Give me that," he said, taking the bowl out of Vicki's hands. He bounded up the steps, and by the time Vicki caught back up with him, he'd rubbed the scrub on the underside of his arm. They stood there and waited.

"How does it feel?" Vicki asked hesitantly. "Is there a tingling sensation?"

"Yeah, it tingles," said Leo. Then he started screaming, "It burns! It burns!"

Vicki gasped and dove for the sink. But Leo burst into uproarious laughter, and she whirled back around.

"You should have seen your face!" Leo crowed. "You actually turned pale."

Vicki's heartbeat slowed its gallop, but she couldn't help a grin. "That was *not* funny. Seriously, how does it feel?"

"It feels really good. It's definitely energizing."

"Good," said Vicki. "I wrote down the measurements, so I should be able to recreate it." She turned on the faucet so Leo could wash his arm, then she splashed him with cold water and bolted down the stairs.

"Now we're even!" she called.

And now she just needed to figure out how to sell those body scrubs . . . before she ran out of time.

Speaking of running out of time . . . Was she forgetting something?

At the bottom of the stairs, she stopped, sniffing. Peppermint still hung heavy in the air, but beneath it was another smell . . . an acrid smell that sent anxiety racing through her body.

Fire? Was the house on fire? Was her house going to burn down just like Mona's store?

She bolted to the kitchen, heart pounding, looking for the source of the flames. Nothing was on fire, but the burning smell was definitely coming from the oven.

"The cornbread!" she wailed.

She grabbed mitts and threw open the oven, coughing at the smoke. Then she pulled out the pan of cornbread and set it down on an open burner. The top was absolutely blackened. She closed the oven slowly, looking mournfully from the ruined cornbread to the clock and back again. She'd forgotten the cornbread in the oven, but it had only been in there an extra couple of minutes.

It might be dry, but it shouldn't be blackened!

She lurched toward the trash and pulled out the box with trembling fingers. "Oh no," she whispered. She'd cooked it at 450 degrees instead of 400. She smacked the box against her head, sending a soft poof of yellow-white powder into the air.

Footfalls behind her announced Leo's arrival. "Everything okay?" he asked, sounding alarmed.

She spun around. "It's fine," she said weakly, "if you weren't too set on having cornbread."

A smirk tugged at the edges of his lips. "I'm not too set on corn-bread if you're not too set on salad."

"Wha—" Her attention snapped to the salad bowl on the counter. A certain white duck was beak-first in the romaine lettuce, looking entirely too satisfied with herself. "Sunny!" she shrieked. "How did you—"

But the answer presented itself immediately when she looked at the window she'd left half-open. "Sunny, did you come in for more blueberries and then decide to eat our salad?"

Leo nodded solemnly. "It appears that's exactly what happened. We can now refer this case to the district attorney."

With a long hiss through her teeth, Vicki said, "Well, we can eat stew? Or order takeout?"

Leo grabbed a spoon and sampled a bite of stew. "The stew will be fine," he declared. "Do you have biscuits or anything to go with it?"

"Mmm, I think I still have some frozen breadsticks we could heat up."

"Perfect."

Ten minutes later, they sat down to a cobbled-together meal of stew and breadsticks. *An odd pairing,* thought Vicki as she took her first bite. *But it works, somehow.*

"So," said Leo. "Grinding the herbs was actually kind of relaxing. Do you need any help getting your things ready to sell at the festival?"

"I was hoping you'd ask," said Vicki. "Would you be able to come over Sunday and help me make a few things?"

"Sure." Leo grabbed a breadstick. "Festival starts soon, doesn't it? I'm happy to help. Just don't make me a guinea pig too often." He stuck his tongue out at her.

She swatted in his direction. Were they still in grade school? But she couldn't keep the grin off her face. "Thank you! I'm so excited! Julia—the woman who hated us—was there today, too, and Kristen *still* let us book a booth."

"Oh?" He made a face. "I thought she wasn't running it this year."

With a shrug, Vicki said, "I guess she's deputy chair now, instead of chair? I'm not clear on the details, but it sounded like maybe her stepdad went around her back and got her demoted so she'd have more time to take care of her sick mom."

Leo chewed on his breadstick and raised his eyebrows. "Really? That's weird."

Vicki recounted the odd argument she'd seen and Kristen's explanation. "Some people are just very insistent on getting their own way, I guess."

"I guess," Leo said. "Oh, that reminds me of this absolutely bizarre case I just finished wrapping up at the station."

They spent the rest of dinner discussing Leo's most recent case. After he left, Vicki cleaned up the dishes and then went into the living room to watch TV. Not that she paid much attention to the show—it mostly hummed in the background as she jotted down ideas for the booth on a yellow legal pad. Finally, after a couple hours, she nodded, satisfied. Mona would have to approve the ideas, but Vicki was sure they'd have a great booth. Her phone dinged with an alert. Someone had placed an order on her online store! She skimmed the order. It was for her sampler package—a small batch of each of her honeys.

Might as well pack that up. She boxed up the honey and addressed it to the customer, then set it on the counter to take to the post office the next day.

After mixing up one more batch of the newly perfected energizing scrub and feeding Sunny, she decided to call it a night.

Just as she was turning out the light to go to bed, her phone rang. It was Leo again.

Vicki furrowed her eyebrows. *Why is he calling so late?* She answered.

"Did you hear what happened?" asked Leo.

Vicki sat up in bed, heart racing. "What's wrong? Are you okay? Is Mona okay?"

"Everyone *you* know is okay. Something happened at the park today. Julia's stepdad died under mysterious circumstances."

He died? I just saw him! "Mysterious circumstances? What happened?" asked Vicki, wide awake now.

"Someone pushed him off the bridge in the park—probably

around two o'clock, we're guessing. There were signs of a struggle. We have Julia's brother in custody."

TO KEEP READING...

*B*ook 2 from Cooking up Murder Available Now...

Click here to get your copy now.

GET SELECT DIANA ORGAIN TITLES FOR FREE

uilding a relationship with my readers is one the things I enjoy best. I occasionally send out messages about new releases, special offers, discount codes and other bits of news relating to my various series.

And for a limited time, I'll send you copy of BUNDLE OF TROUBLE: Book 1 in the MATERNAL INSTINCTS MYSTERY SERIES.

Join now

OTHER TITLES BY DIANA ORGAIN

Third Time's a Crime If only love were as simple as murder...

Yappy Hour Things take a *ruff* turn at the Wine & Bark when Maggie Patterson takes charge

Trigger Yappy Salmonella poisoning strikes at the Wine & Bark.

A Witch Called Wanda Can a witch solve a murder mystery?

I Wanda put a spell on you When Wanda is kidnapped, Maeve might need a little magic.

Brewing up Murder A witch, a murder, a dog...no, wait...a man..no...two men, three witches and a cat?

Murder as Sticky as Jam Mona and Vicki are ready for the grand opening of Jammin' Honey until...their store goes up in smoke...

Murder as Sweet as Honey Will the sweet taste of honey turn bitter with a killer town?

Murder as Savory as Biscuits Can some savory biscuits uncover the truth behind a murder?

ABOUT THE AUTHOR

*D*iana Orgain is the bestselling author of the *Maternal Instincts Mystery Series,* the *Love or Money Mystery Series,* and the *Roundup Crew Mysteries.* She is the co-author of NY Times Best-selling *Scrapbooking Mystery Series* with Laura Childs. For a complete listing of books, as well as excerpts and contests, and to connect with Diana:

Visit Diana's website at www.dianaorgain.com.

Join Diana reader club and newsletter and get Free books here

Made in United States
Orlando, FL
08 September 2024

51275619R00086